PUFFIN BOOKS

THE FUTURE-TELLING L...

In this captivating collection of stories, James Berry conjures up an exciting variety of moods. Affectionately humorous: cheeky Boy-Don takes a trip on the banana truck to visit Granny-May, but we see a different side of his character when he experiences terrible homesickness. Quietly eerie: Sherena shakes hands with a ghost down at Cotton-Tree. Intriguing: the future-telling lady reveals the grown-up diaries of the troubled children who are sent to her for advice. Dark and haunting: the personal tragedy of Ajeemah and his son sold into slavery and separated from each other provides the focus for a vivid and authentic account of a brutal plantation slave society.

All of the stories in this collection are in their own way thrilling to read. Richly evocative, sometimes surprising, together they make a memorable collection.

James Berry was born and brought up in Jamaica, and now divides his time between Jamaica and the United Kingdom. He is a distinguished writer and has published poems and short stories in the United States, Britain and the Caribbean. In 1987 he was the Grand Prix Winner of the Smarties Prize for his collection of short stories, *A Thief in the Village*, and in 1989 he received the Signal Poetry Award for his collection of poems, *When I Dance*. In 1991 he won the Cholmondely Award for poetry given by the Society of Authors. In 1990 he was awarded the OBE for his services to poetry.

The FUTURE-TELLING LADY

Seven Stories by
JAMES BERRY

PUFFIN BOOKS

For my father,
called Cousin Oldmaster

PUFFIN BOOKS

Published by the Penguin Group
Penguin Books Ltd, 27 Wrights Lane, London W8 5TZ, England
Penguin Books USA Inc., 375 Hudson Street, New York, New York 10014, USA
Penguin Books Australia Ltd, Ringwood, Victoria, Australia
Penguin Books Canada Ltd, 10 Alcorn Avenue, Toronto, Ontario, Canada M4V 3B2
Penguin Books (NZ) Ltd, 182–190 Wairau Road, Auckland 10, New Zealand

Penguin Books Ltd, Registered Offices: Harmondsworth, Middlesex, England

First published by Hamish Hamilton Ltd 1991
Published in Puffin Books 1993
3 5 7 9 10 8 6 4 2

Text copyright © James Berry, 1991
All rights reserved

The moral right of the author has been asserted

Printed in England by Clays Ltd, St Ives plc
Set in Palatino

Contents

Cotton-Tree Ghosts

It was Sunday. It was a very bright, glassy, sun-hot day in Flametree Village. The village was settled along the edge of one big cattle-rearing estate. Long ago, all this piece of Jamaica was Arawak Indians' land. Then white landowners, Afro-Caribbean people and a few Asian people lived here. Now mostly Afro-Caribbean people lived in the settlement that became Flametree Village.

Today, most people had gone to church. Those at home lounged about quietly on verandas or under backyard trees, reading the Bible or just snoozing. No wonder Flametree Village was having its special Sunday-quiet. The feeling of mystery in the day had a wide loneliness you couldn't escape — that amazing Sunday-atmosphere! But, out of it all, out of this day so imbued with holiness, something else, something most unexpected, happened.

Sherena Bignal was on the front veranda, writing up her school work. She looked up, looked round, stood up. And leaving her exercise book with her pen in it, and her notes pages opened, Sherena went quietly, tiptoeing about. She saw her father sleeping with the Bible beside him in the cool of the creeper-grown back veranda. She saw her mother stretched out asleep on her bed, under the gently-moving curtains at the window.

Sherena left the house like a quiet flutter of breeze. She carried her red-patterned raffia bag, empty, over her shoulder. In her thin white dress, a floppy blue hat and blue canvas shoes, she was noticeable. But nobody was about to see her. She simply walked on nippily. And her neat and slender feet took her quickly in the quiet and hot sunny day. A short way along, Sherena turned off the village road. She was amazed how there wasn't a single other human movement or sound anywhere. And she loved it. She opened the gate, closed it and came into the big cattle pasture.

On Friday, the pasture was emptied of its cattle, taken elsewhere. Sherena's excitement bounced up a bit more; she'd seen an almond tree. But she ignored this one. The tree was small and unreliable. She remembered that this year the tree had no almonds at all.

Her craving for almonds sharpened. Soon, she'd collect her bagful! Take them back, break them open, and have a feast, eating them with coconut. Then drink a cool, cool glass of lemonade. Oh, what joy! Made your mouth water just thinking of it! Good thing she knew exactly where those two fabulous almond trees were. All loaded with green almonds hanging. All scattered around with dropped ripe nuts!

Sherena came to the sharp and gritty slope. Unexpectedly, she saw what seemed part of old ruins. Then she noticed what could have been an old entrance. She stepped closer. Almost hidden, covered with vines, under a tree branch, it could be the ruins of an ancient gateway pillar. Sherena was surprised. It seemed so mysterious! How's it she never seen it before? And not even known it exists? And the numberless times she'd been here! And, passed here! Then, thinking of her almonds, the pillar went out of her head. She stepped off again knowing that the gritty slope led up to a surprising flat of grassland. And best of all, her two enormously towering and spreading almond trees were there. And some flame-trees were there too, spreading themselves even wider than the almond trees. Then, standing quite apart, there was the fantastic, thick and wide based Cotton-Tree. Its vast trunk tapered up and up majestically, as if it wanted its top to touch the sky.

She came up to the top of the slope, with all her thoughts concentrated purely on collecting her bagful of almond nuts. Sherena knew the land very well. Her head down, she walked on hurriedly, thinking of exactly what she was going to do. Then, with a smile on her face, Sherena looked up to greet her fabulous almond trees. The smile disappeared from her face. Her almond trees weren't there! Weren't there! The flame-trees weren't there! Sherena looked round and round. She saw a big old house with gardens and old-fashioned white people. 'The whole place is different!' she whispered. 'What's happened? Jesu! Am I lost? The place is somewhere else. I'm at strange people's place. Hope they don't have bad dogs. Hope I don't get in trouble. Where, where am I?' It flashed through Sherena's head she must be dreaming. But she couldn't remember lying down anywhere to go to sleep. She was glad nobody

seemed to see her. She stood looking at the old-
fashioned white gentlemen and white ladies, eating.
Picnicking under the great Cotton-Tree! She watched.
The people ate, drank, joked and laughed. It was all
very strange. Almost with a shock, she noticed the
children — all white children — playing about. Mostly
girls — in long old-fashioned clothes with lots of
ribbons. Some of them rolled hoops along and ran
behind them, striking the hoops with a stick to keep
them going. Other children played with a cup and a
ball attached. The ball was tossed up and caught in
the cup. Totally engrossed, Sherena stood watching,
knowing she didn't want to be seen. She didn't know
how she'd get away.

From nowhere, an older girl stood in front of her.
And the strange, freckled-face girl, with long, untidy
blonde hair, stretched her hand out to her. As they
clasped hands, the girl said, 'How do you do?'

'I'm well,' Sherena answered.

'I know you are,' the strange girl said.

Amazed, Sherena said, 'You know me?'

'I know who you are.'

Sherena stared into the freckled face and slowly
shook her head. 'No. No. I dohn know you at all. From
when and where you got to know me?'

'Ah! I'll inform you of the connection. You are the
offspring of your father's great-grandfather's father and
his grandfather, who was William, our coachman.'

'William?'

'Yes, William. He brought us here every end-of-
week. You see, still, we love it here.'

'Children!' somebody called. 'Children! Come on!'

'That's Mother. I must go. My name is Magdalen. Goodbye.'

Sherena looked. All the people had moved. And everything cleared up! In a flash, there was nobody! She looked round. She barely caught a glimpse of a carriage vanishing through the old gateway. She stood stunned. All was like the puzzle of a dream. An almond fell from the tree and dropped at her feet. Dreamily, she looked at the browny-yellow husk of the nut, shaped like a small egg. She looked up again. Everything had come back to normal! She saw — every tree, every thing, was there, in place, as she knew the land.

A terror whipped round Sherena and gripped her. She nearly fainted. She saved herself with her dread, her terrible horror, of being alone. Instead of fainting, she hit the Sunday-quiet, cutting through the day with 'Mamma!' And Sherena ran. She found herself running like crazy. She ran on and on, calling, 'Mamma!' as if a monster chased her.

When Sherena's mum heard her alarmed voice, she was already in the yard. Breathless, she crashed into her mother's arms in the sitting-room. 'Wha's the matter? Wha's the matter?' Mrs Bignal said. Her father rushed up, looking as anxious as her mother, who begged her, 'Calm down, Shere. Calm down. Please.'

Sherena thrashed about. 'Mamma, I saw ghosts! I saw ghosts!'

'Calm yourself, now. Calm yourself!'

'Shere? You seen ghosts?' Mr Bignal said excitedly.

'Yes, Daddy. Yes!'

'Where? Where you seen ghosts?'

'At almond trees, where I go to get almonds.'

'Tha's not almond tree. Tha's Cotton-Tree! Round middleday now — Sunday. Girl, you seen Cotton-Tree Ghosts! Easy. They harmless.'

'You feeling better?' her mother asked.

'Yes, Mam.'

'Come. Si-down. Si-down, now.'

'I'm still alive, Mam?'

The parents laughed. 'Yes, sweetheart,' her mother said. 'You still very much alive.'

'Dohn laugh, Mam. Feel my hand. Feel it. Is it ahright?'

'I feeling it. Is ahright.'

'I'm alive, yes?'

'Of course you're alive.'

'Mam, I shake hands with a ghost!'

'Huh-huh!' Mr Bignal said. 'You actually shake hands with Magdalen?'

'Yeahs! You know about Magdalen, Dad? She's known about?'

'Yes, Sherena. Magdalen is known about. She always wahn to shake hands. And she always leaves her name. She did, didn' she?'

'Yeahs!' Sherena sat up crossly. 'Then how's it I knew nothing? Nothing — about Cotton-Tree Ghosts? Nobody ever said a word!'

'Children dohn know these things these days,' her mother said. 'It's — it's a long long time since anybody mentioned the ghosts.'

'They always come at middleday, then?'

'Yeh,' said Mr Bignal. 'And on a Sunday. People who see them always see them around twelve a'clock – on Sunday, when all quiet. When the hot middleday sunlight a-shimmer. And nobody about. And there's no human noise. Only bird-singing. And occasional animal cry. And the ghosts come. And bring all another world altogether! Fantastic!' Sherena's dad became thoughtful. Then he went on, 'And, Shere – you saw – actually saw – the whole family?'

'Yeahs, Dad! The whole white family and friends! With children playing about. Incredible! Incredible! Is a dream you will never forget! And I knew nothing. Knew nothing about these incredible visitors!'

'They harmless, sweetheart. Harmless. I tell you, I envy you. I never seen them. As a young fellow, I spent many Sundays at Cotton-Tree, waiting to see the white people ghosts. And get a handshake from Magdalen. But nothing! Jus' cahn see them.'

'Magdalen told me she knew who I was.'

'Huh-huh! Did she?'

'She said, she could inform me of my connection.'

'Huh-huh!' her dad said. 'Go on then.'

'She said – wait, I must remember this – said, "You are the offspring of your father's great-grandfather's father and his grandfather, who was William, our coach-man."'

'Fantastic!'

'Dad, did you know about a coachman William – going way back?'

'No. Not at all. Not at all. But – I'll tell you – '

'Isn' there something,' Mrs Bignal said, 'about the

whole family drowning in the sea-flood of the Port Royal earthquake?'

'Yeh, yeh. I was going to say that.'

'That was the earthquake of 1692,' Sherena said, 'that destroyed our town of Port Royal?'

'Correct,' Mr Bignal said, 'correct. The story goes that the ol' man of the ghost family used to be wealthy. It goes that he was a merchant and a law man at Port Royal. And along with his town house, he owned the land here with its big country house.'

'Yes, yes!' Sherena said. 'Magdalen said William used to drive them in their carriage to their country house, at the end-of-week.'

'Fascinating. Also,' Mr Bignal said, 'the story goes that the whole family died having lunch. Drowned suddenly, in the crazy ringing of church bells, as the earthquake broke up the churches. And the bells all ringing their own ring till the sea swallowed them.'

'What did the ghosts women look like?' Mrs Bignal asked.

'Old fashioned,' Sherena said. 'All old fashioned. All puffed sleeves, long blown-out dresses. And ribbons, ribbons, ribbons!'

'And the men?'

'Straight, oily-looking long hair, parted in the middle. And handlebar moustaches with a pointed twist at the end.'

'Shere, sweetheart,' Mr Bignal said, 'how did it actually feel, shaking hands with a ghost?'

Sherena shivered. 'Dad, Dad, dohn remind me. Dohn remind me, please, please! Is too horrible now.' She looked at her hand. 'Hand, you held a ghost. You ahright? You not turned white or shrivelled up or something?'

Her dad insisted. 'Sweetheart, when there holding on to Magdalen's hand, did it feel like air, or an ordinary hand or what?'

'Oh, Dad! It was all ordinary, Like meeting any stranger. The awful awful horrors come on afterwards. Like now.'

'Her voice – how did that sound?'

'Her voice?'

'Yes.'

'When it was happening I expected it the way it sounded. Now – I imagine, her voice, like, very very ancient royal family voice. Ever so, ever so, loaded. With everything extra.'

'Bet you, Sherena,' her mother said, 'you not going again to pick up almonds when you dohn go church?'

'Me, mam? Oh, Lord have mercy! Never! Not on a Sunday. Not anytime at Cotton-Tree. Me one not ever going to that place again!'

'Dohn worry,' her dad said. 'Is all harmless if you dohn worry.'

'Why?' Sherena asked. 'Dad, why d'you think the ghosts leave from wherever they are to come back here?'

'Dohn know, Shere, sweetheart. Maybe – they attached to the place. They like to come back. Maybe – because once the white people belonged to here – they always part of it. Who knows?'

Magic to Make You Invisible

That Julian had too much time for himself! She had too little time for herself, to do what she liked. Now — Saturday morning — she was left to clean the house. Nothing about this was fair.

Yuuni dusted and tidied up, feeling really cross. Puppa was gone to help another man with some work. Mumma, as usual, took vegetables, fruits and eggs to the town market to sell. And what about her younger brother, Julian? Wasn't the Mr Julian gone sea swimming? With friends? Just as he did every Saturday morning? So, alone, she was house-cleaning. Isn't it great, how something like a miracle has happened, that will change everything. Everything!

Every time — well, nearly every time — Puppa talked to Julian, Puppa put his arm around him. Nearly every time Puppa came home, out from his pocket came sweets, or something, for who? For Julian. Mumma did about the same, adding a kiss. They hardly remember she was there. Hardly they even think of her, the girl Yuuni, the older one twelve years old. Her parents took no notice of that. In the same way they took no notice Julian was her most hurtful problem. Now, they'll know nothing that she'd found a way to deal with her problem.

Yuuni stopped cleaning the mirror. She stopped as

she remembered she'd woken up this morning with the most fantastic dream in her head. She'd rushed to the Bible. She'd opened the Bible and rustled through the thin leaves quick, quick. And there it was. The exact verse from her dream was correct. It was right. She knew now everything, everything else, would work. Funny how everybody always said she was like her father. And she was really turning out to be a miracle dreamer like him. Full of thinking, Yuuni sat down.

Only weeks ago, her Puppa's dream won him fifty thousand dollars. He'd dreamed the number of the lottery ticket. Seen the exact number in his dream! And it won top prize — all that mighty lot of money. Now she herself had dreamed something mighty big. She'd dreamed how to make Julian invisible. Yuuni giggled: Julian totally invisible! And she remembered everything in the dream. Everything! Thinking of the magic, Yuuni actually gave a shiver. Her slim body shook. Her heartbeat went faster. The strange magic feeling scared her. But the peculiar feeling also gave her exciting sensations. 'Julian totally invisible,' echoed in her head. She giggled again, got up and went on with her work.

Julian came home happily, on his bicycle. He came whistling into the open, airy and sunlit little bungalow. Yuuni heard and saw him. Then she heard him searching the kitchen and dining room but stayed quiet, thinking, 'Listen to that bossy greedy guts! As usual turning the place upside-down for food after enjoying himself!'

Julian came out on to the veranda, eating. He carried

thick pieces of bun and cheese on a plate, and a mug of iced lemonade he'd mixed. Changed into his white shirt with the lion-head printed on the chest, he put everything on the little table, sat down and went on eating. Yuuni came out too, barefeet, carrying a glass of lemonade. Her string-waisted skirt and short blouse left Yuuni's midriff bare. She leaned forward and said, 'Something fantastic happened, Julian!'

Julian looked up. 'Yeh?' Mixed cheese, bun and lemonade filled his mouth.

'You know Puppa's dream won him that pile of money?'

'Yeh, yeh.'

'And it made his picture get in the newspapers?'

'Yeh.'

'And it made him buy us new things, though mostly you — with a new room being built on the house for you and all.'

'Well, well — okay. Okay.'

'And people, even strangers, come to the house smiling at him, hoping to get a dollar or two? And some do?'

'Yeh.'

'Well — last night — I myself had a dream. A magic dream.'

Julian was excited. 'You dream a lottery number, too!'

'No. Something else.'

'What? What, Yuuni?'

'I dream how to make somebody invisible.'

Julian went dumb for some seconds. Then pieces of

hot potatoes seemed to come into his mouth when he tried to speak. 'In -vi -vi -vi -visible? Can't be seen?'

Yuuni nodded. 'Yes. That's it. Have it in my head right now.'

'Right now you have that trick in you?'

'How to make somebody transparent? Totally transparent? So no eyes can see him? All here in my head.'

'But, Yuuni — thas magic! Thas bigger — much bigger — than Puppa's fifty thousand dollars. You're mightier, a mightier dreamer than Puppa.'

'It gets me like that, too.'

Julian popped his eyes. 'What you going to do with it?'

Yuuni was cool. 'I'm talking to you. Nobody else.'

Julian got up and walked a half circle. 'Yuuni — Sista Yuuni — we could work wonders!'

'Like what?'

Julian clenched his fists and held them tight. 'Yuuni, this is fantasplosive.' He used one of his made-up big words that his friends used back to him. 'Fantasplosive,' he repeated. And more of his own language followed. 'This is real sensation dizzy-dizzy. You going tell anybody?'

'You think I'm stupid. I'm only telling you.'

'Wow, wow, whoopey! What a whoopey!'

'You'll have to help me to make it work, Julian.'

'Help you? I'm your partner. Let's make it work now. Let's try it out. Try it out, right away.'

'Not yet. Not yet. You can only see how it works as we go along.'

'Okay, then. Okay.'

'What would you like to do with this magic, yourself?'

'Wow! No end to it, Yuuni.'

'What, for example?'

'Well — first of all — you know that boy Lester Davis?'

'Yeh.'

'Lester Davis is always tripping me up and go on all sorry like. It'd be a fantasplosion keeping on tripping him up. And he can see nobody. Nobody who's doing it. Then all those sudden backslappers. Boy, wouldn't I surprise them. They're having a serious conversation and whack! and whack! in the middle of the back. Wow! Then, then, with this magic, I can pick my lessons. Those I hate, I just show up to be seen. Then, I'm not there.'

'Anything else?'

'Just once — one time only — it'd be a wow to shove Lester Davis in front of the Headmaster as he's passing us kids, to see the two tangled up on the ground together.' Julian laughed with enjoyment. Yuuni couldn't help laughing too. 'But, the best, best joke,' Julian went on, 'would be picking cakes off the cake-seller tray at schoolyard. Just to see her face, as one by one every cake disappears from her tray.' Julian laughed. 'Fantasplosion! She'd die, wouldn't she? They'd have to get the First Aid kit.'

'What about house-cleaning, dish-washing, food preparing for cooking, and all that?'

'Yeh, yeh. You yourself could baffle Mumma. Couldn't you? And same way with me. When they want me do a job, I just disappear. I'm nowhere. Though was just there. Just there! They call; I'm nowhere.' Excitement in his eyes, Julian grinned. 'Sensation, oh sensation! Yuuni, come on. Let's start up the magic. Mumma and Puppa not here till later. It's a good time.'

'I can't tell you anything before we're doing it. Understand? So don't ask, don't insist, don't do anything to spoil anything. Right?'

Julian raised his opened hands to Yuuni, in submission and agreement, and said, 'I swear. I swear to be obedient.'

'Right. I can tell you a little bit, now. Monday's a school holiday. That'll make everything perfect. We need today, tomorrow and Monday. That is, from today to twelve o'clock on the third day. We have to be careful to turn things on midday on the third day. We must.'

'Okay. I know three is a magic number. I know that.'

'You know that?'

'Yeh.'

'Jesus died at the age of thirty-three at three o'clock. Did you know that?'

'No. I didn't know that.'

'There you are. You don't know everything.'

'My leader, I follow. I'm jobless for a job.'

'You'll have to catch three dragonflies.'

'Three Needlepoints? As part of the magic?'

'As part of the preparation.'

'Oh, boy! Big job. Any questions allowed?'

'No questions allowed.'

'Well — I'll have to get some gum.'

'Will take too long to tap a tree for gum.'

'I think — I think I could get some gum from Benji.'

'Then, go and get the gum from Benji.'

Julian wheeled away on his bicycle. It didn't take him long to come back with some tacky gum in a piece of coconut shell. 'I'll go and set the gum for the Needlepoints,' he told Yunni.

'Okay. Set the gum, leave it and come back.'

Again Julian wheeled away off on his bicycle. At the pond in the pasture, swarms of dragonflies and butterflies flew over and around the pool of water, and were also perched on the dry tops of stems and other water plants. Bare twiggy tops of stems were places to set the gum. Julian set his gum traps and came back home.

'I'm ready for our next job,' Yunni said. 'See I've got my shoes on.'

'Information needed,' Julian said. 'What's this job?'

'Getting three ratbats.'

'Ratbats?'

'Yeh.'

'They're ugly, awful, disgusting creatures! And live in a cave.'

'All true. But we must get three of them.'

'You'll have to do the catching and the holding them,' Julian said.

'Ahright,' Yuuni said. 'I'll do the catching. I'll hold them. And we've got to be quick. We got to get back before Mumma or Puppa gets home.'

'Bottomwood Caves not too far.'

'That's right. We go there.'

Yuuni and Julian walked across the cow pasture. They came along and heard the sea. Then they climbed the leafy, creeper-covered rocky hillside facing the sea. Yuuni leading the way, they turned into a cave entrance and went on in.

Julian turned on the torch and moved the shining light about. The dark stinking underground space went on all round. Bats hung, head downwards, asleep, singly or in clusters. Julian thought this must have been a burial place for some Arawak Indians long long time ago. As he and his sister moved on into the dark, smelly and scary cave, their feet kept sinking into ages of bat droppings.

'Beginning of hell this,' Julian whispered. 'Creepy as worms.'

'Horrible,' Yuuni whispered back. 'But we won't be long.'

Julian stopped. 'I go no further. Snakes, scorpions, everything, must be here. Satan himself could suddenly collar you here.'

'There, look! Some together just overhead here.'

A couple of steps and light held closely on the sleeping brown bats made them give a little dozy shiver. A towel in her hand, the determined Yuuni grabbed a bunch of the hanging bats and stuffed them in the white pillowcase she carried. Outside the cave, they checked. Yuuni had grabbed exactly three bats. Going home, Yuuni and Julian stopped at the pond and also collected up exactly three trapped dragonflies.

At home, Yuuni smiled to herself. Everything has

worked well. Totally well! Full success with everything is a good, good sign. But, more things had to be
done.

Yuuni sent Julian off again. He came back with three
white wing-feathers from a village man's white pigeon.
And now it was time to get everything together that
made the magic.

Yuuni tied up the three bats in one white handkerchief and the three dragonflies in another. She put three
cups of water in a saucepan, and then put in the encased
bats and dragonflies. She covered the saucepan and let
it boil three-quarters of an hour. Keeping strict time,
Yuuni poured off the magic liquid stock from the
saucepan into a jug and put it in a safe place to
cool. She then made Julian bury the cooked bats and
dragonflies, with a little wooden cross over them.

The magic stock cooled and Yuuni put it into a
drinking glass. Out of her pocket, she took a page torn
out from the Bible; it was the whole page of Psalm 3.
She folded the Bible page into three, and carefully let
it stand in the magic stock in the glass. She put the
drinking glass with everything in a bigger jar, and put
the three white feathers to stand outside the glass in
the jar. She placed a wooden cross on top of the glass
and carefully fitted on the lid of the jar. Finally, taking
great care, Yuuni and Julian buried the jar and marked
the spot with a heavy stone.

To have to wait till the third day for the working
of the magic was the hardest test for Yuuni and Julian.
Though excited and impatient, Julian slept well. Twice
Yuuni woke up, and giggled at the thought of turning

Julian invisible. It unexpectedly struck Yuuni that, when Julian became invisible, she wouldn't know how to make him real again. That wasn't in the dream. Well – she'd have to take a chance on that. Something would make him come back real, at some time. As long as she could make him invisible when she liked, that was what mattered.

On the second day, in the evening, Julian whispered to Yuuni, 'The stone's still there in place.'

She answered quietly. 'I know.'

Twelve o'clock Monday, at the end of the backyard, Yuuni and Julian dug up their secret magic jar. Yuuni held the glass with the cross on it. She looked unblinking into Julian's eyes and said, 'At my command, when this drink is drunk, and has disappeared, Julian, you will be unseeable.' She removed the cross from the top of the glass, stepped forward, and made the sign of the cross on Julian's forehead. She handed him the glass and said, 'Drink this drink, Julian.'

Julian took the magic drink. He lifted the glass and swallowed down the cold and nasty brothy soup and winced. He stood blinking hard, testing himself to see how he felt. Sensation dizzy-dizzy now! Was he normal? 'Can you see me?' he asked.

'First time – I can't tell,' Yuuni said. 'We have to try it out on somebody else.'

'Really?' Julian said, sounding and looking as if he didn't know whether he was really alive or not.

'Let's go and see if Mumma can see you.'

Julian looked doubtful about what to do, but said, 'Okay. I'll see if Mumma can see me.'

'Go carefully, like. Carefully,' Yuuni said unnecessarily.

Julian walked up from the backyard, feeling and looking like a zombie. He went into the kitchen, trying to creep up quietly on his mother, who stood at the table preparing lunch. Half hiding, Yuuni stood in the doorway.

'What the devil you come creeping up behind me about?' his mother said crossly. 'What you playing at? Eh? I was looking for you, anyway. Take the bucket and get a couple of buckets of water. And where's that sister of yours? Eh? Where's she?'

Fantasplosion! The magic didn't work! After all that trouble! Yet all over himself Julian felt a great, great relief. The taste of the nasty magic soup was still in his mouth. He picked up the bucket. He went out to get water from the standing-pipe at the roadside. Yuuni slunk into the kitchen, feeling really down with disappointment. She sighed sadly, but began helping her mother.

Yet, if Yuuni's mother had known what she and her brother had done to the helpless bats and dragonflies, Yuuni wouldn't only have sighed. Her mother would have made her cry. But, who could tell? When the parents found the missing Bible leaf, and all was revealed, who could say what might happen?

Julian took a long time coming back with the water. His mother was suddenly concerned. Right away Yuuni said she'd go and find him. She rushed out and ran up the road.

Nobody was at the roadside standing-pipe, only

Julian's bucket. Yuuni clasped her face in shock. 'Julian!' she whispered nervously, looking all around. 'Are you here?' She stretched out her arms, moving round and round, feeling the air, to see if Julian was there. 'Julian?' She stood. 'Julian? Are you here? Somewhere?'

No answer. Yuuni was frightened. Then she heard coughing. Someone was being sick. Where did the coughing come from? Yuuni listened carefully. The throwing-up coughing went again. Yuuni spun herself round. Where? Where did it come from? It could have come from anywhere, she thought. 'It's happened,' she whispered. 'He's gone invisible! But the magic mixture is making him sick ... Perhaps he could die. Suppose he died?' Tears came quickly into Yunni's eyes. She hugged herself tightly. 'Oh God, my brother's bodyless! Dear God, Dear God, give him back a body to go with his voice. Do, give him back his body to go with his voice. Do ...'

Yuuni looked and saw Julian climbing over the property wall he'd hidden behind. 'Julian,' she said, 'you've tricked me!'

'I was being sick, and saw you coming. I was thinking Mumma would follow. So I jumped over the wall.'

'So you're back!' Yuuni said. She turned and walked off crossly, thinking, 'He's back! We'll have to do it all over again. And make it work. Make it work.'

Banana-Day Trip

'Boy-Don, you're dressed up and ready!' Playfully teasing, big brother Andy stared at him. 'You all ready to go to Granny!'

There on the front veranda, brushing down his dog, Boy-Don was cool. 'Yes. I'm ready. And, man, I kind-a could like no problems from you. Telling me I'm too early. Or anything like that.'

Acting all repentant, fourteen-year-old Andy put his hands together, as if he was praying, asking forgiveness. He shook his head. 'No. No, Boy-Don! You want to be two hours early. I would *never* be the one to interfere one bit.'

Boy-Don called out loudly, 'Mamma? Mamma?'

'Yeahs!' His mum answered from a side room of the sprawling bungalow. Both Mrs and Mr Wallman were head teachers. Though it was school holidays, they were over papers at their desks in the house, working.

'Is it true, Mamma, I have to wait two hours?'

'Not true. Ignore your brother, Andy.'

'You think, Mamma — per'aps — Mr Burke forgot to call for me?'

'No, Boy-Don. Mr Burke won't forget. Just be patient.'

Boy-Don gave Andy one cross look and went on slowly brushing down his dog, Browndash. Before

Andy could say anything else, their dad called him to go and do a job. Looking at his young brother, Andy went with his face full of a teasing smile. What Andy didn't know was that as he turned his back, Boy-Don also had a glint of happy mischief in his eye. He knew Andy and Hannah were jealous over his trip alone to Granny. For him, Boy-Don, their jealousy made his going away bigger, more exciting, more special, more stupendous.

Dressed in his cleaned sneakers, his fresh blue denim trousers, denim short-sleeved shirt and denim long peaked cap turned sideways on his head, Boy-Don brushed his dog. But he kept his ears cocked sharp. All the time he listened. He listened to pick out the distant horn-blowing of Mr Burke's loaded banana-truck that would take him to Granny-May's house. He'd stay there one whole week!

From nowhere, twelve-year-old Hannah popped out on to the veranda. She sat down in a deckchair. Boy-Don said, 'My sister — you come to keep me company, or to trouble me?'

'Why you so impatient to get away?'

'I'm not on my way to Granny yet. Mr Burke's taking ages getting me away from you.'

'Boy-Don, I was thinking. I had to come and talk to you. D'you know exactly why *you* are going to stay with Granny-May and not me? Or Andy? Or Mark?'

Boy-Don tossed his arms about. 'Jealous! Jealous! Jealous!'

'Favouritism! That's what it is. Favouritism!'

Boy-Don stood with Browndash and faced Hannah

crossly. 'Granny-May love me best. She love me best. Me is the one she love best.'

'Listen to him! Listen to him! Can't even talk properly. If Mamma could hear you. Don't you know when to say, "Granny-May *loves* me best"? Instead of "love", "loves me best"? And haven't you learnt yet how to say, "I am the one she *loves* best"? Instead of "me", "me is the one"?'

Boy-Don frowned in a scared way, looking round. He didn't want their mum to hear at all. 'Ahright! Ahright!' he said in a hushed voice. 'Next time I say it properly. Next time. Next time.'

'All that bad-talk. Taking all that bad-talk to Granny-May! See now why I'd be the fit person to go for the week? See now?'

'You know lots of things already. Lots of things what correct. I'll benefit. I'll learn something.'

'There you go again. There you go with "lots of things what correct". You must say, "lots of things *that are* correct".'

'You could make me go wrong and go wrong and go wrong by telling me, telling me all the time I'm wrong.'

'I'm trying to point out to you something all obvious. If I was the one going to Granny-May I'd have a lot, lot more that's interesting to say there, and say when I get back. Understand that?'

Boy-Don turned to brushing his dog again. 'You'll see if I don't have lots, lots that's interesting when I get back.'

'We'll see. We will all see. I know. I get it.'

'Get what?'

'Your big thing in mind is to do rap rhymes about Granny-May.'

Boy-Don protested. 'No! Granny-May is the best. I would never pull a joke on Granny-May. Never! That's what I do to you. But never Granny-May.'

'I should've asked Granny-May to let me come along to look after you. You know that?'

Offended like a teased dog, Boy-Don turned round swiftly and yapped. 'You crazy? You mad? Who'd want you to come? You not dumb. You know when somebody is specially invited and when somebody else specially *not* invited.'

'I had to pack your bag for you.'

'And I had to stop you putting in school books and too much clothes.'

'Going to wear your cap front-sideways at Granny's?'

'My business, Hannah! My business!' He turned his back on her.

She leapt up. 'Okay. If you're going to be rude, I'll just go.'

'And great riddance.'

'We'll see what you have to say that's of any interest whatsoever when you get back. We'll just wait and see!' And Hannah was gone.

There was a kind of mock-cross affection between Hannah and Boy-Don. They argued a lot. Hannah would never admit how much Boy-Don's rap rhymes and performances amused her. She called his rap rhymes 'silly forced-ripe verse'. Yet she'd get at him, set him up, to perform, making it look as if it was for their dad. The first time that Boy-Don excitedly got everybody together to hear his rap rhymes, Hannah whispered to herself, 'Fantastic! Brilliant!' Wide-eyed, she'd been amazed he could do what he did. Hannah would never let on that, getting Boy-Don to do it for her over and over, she'd memorised every word. And standing in front of the mirror, she'd practised and imitated his style. She only had to think of it, close her eyes and there was Boy-Don performing.

Cap-peak turned sideways over his ear, head nodding, arms swinging in strict-rhythm dance, his poem comes from memory —

> I'm the boy called Boy-Don
> well known as number one style man
> with only that bother of a sister
> and each of the other called brother.
>
> But I done them in with new-craze.
> I leave them in oldtime days
> the way me one wear my cap
> with my style of rap.
>
> Everywhere people like to see me,
> everywhere people like to hear me,
> this boy called Boy-Don
> the number one style man
>   the number one style man ...

All as excited as he was about going away, Boy-Don had not forgotten his jobs he had to do. One by one he'd done what he could. What he couldn't finish he fixed up for somebody to do while he was away. These jobs were to do with animals given to him by relatives. His goat he called 'Goaty'; his pig he called 'Rhino'; his dog, of course, he called 'Browndash'. He gave each animal its own special care. He used to ride the pig and goat around the yard. When he was lying down on the veranda, drawing or writing his rap rhymes, Boy-Don would have Goaty, Rhino and Browndash lying down on the floor around him.

His going away made him work for them. For some days he'd spent his time cutting grass, bringing it and piling it up for Goaty, to eat while he was away. Andy had promised to give Goaty some of the special grass daily — saying it was from Boy-Don. He'd also prepared special feed for Rhino. Again, Andy promised he'd feed the pig, telling it was from Boy-Don. Hannah had promised she'd give Browndash his special dog bits, saying Boy-Don left them for him. Nobody had to bathe the dog. Boy-Don had done that himself yesterday.

Boy-Don called loudly, 'Mamma? ... Mamma? ... Mamma?'

At last his mum answered, 'Yeahs!'

'Mr Burke isn't coming for me.'

'Yeahs — he will. Just wait. And please don't bother me.'

That reassurance cheered up Boy-Don. He sat down comfortably in a deckchair with his dog and travel bag beside him. He'd been thinking perhaps he really should have gone on either a mini-bus or the big bus. *But*, it was Mr Burke's banana-truck he'd begged his parents to let him go with. It was great how he lived near a banana plantation and near a banana packing-house, how Mr Burke was a neighbour, how he was a planter himself and owner-driver of a banana-truck. And his great truck carried bananas to the wharf for ships that carried them overseas to different, different cities of the world! To think that bananas he knew and watched develop should travel to cities overseas pleased, thrilled and fascinated him no end.

Hannah came back and pretended to be ever so surprised. 'Oh, Mr Big-Talk Traveller is still here!' The sound of Hannah's words became mixed with the horn-blowing of a distant truck.

Boy-Don leapt up, shouting. 'He's coming! He's coming! Mr Burke's coming!' He dashed inside, kissed his mum, dashed to another room, kissed his dad and was outside again, bag in hand. The big, long, loaded truck stopped in a fanfare of horn-blowing at the gate. Its load was covered with a green tarpaulin. It kept its engine running while the whole family came out. Boy-Don climbed up, went in the cab and sat beside Mr Burke. In its ear-splitting horn-blowing, the truck drove off. Everybody waved goodbye. Boy-Don waved back, feeling great. At that moment he didn't mind at all if he never came back, ever.

Boy-Don's head moved from side to side, looking through the windscreen of the truck and its open windows. The fields of coconut trees that they passed, like the grazing cattle pasture, looked all different from inside the cab of a loaded, moving banana-truck.

The smiler-face Mr Burke was quite a talker. 'Banana-Day gets the fields and packing-house lively and bustling. And the trucks on the road. Eh, Boy-Don?'

'Yes, sir. Some people get money.'

'You know it, man. You know it.'

'Yes.'

'When I was your age, a banana market-day was different.'

'Different, sir?'

'Oh, yeh. Those days, whole village goes a-bustle with banana-selling. Mostly everybody sells a bunch or two. Bananas come from mountain-land, lowland, yard-land — all about — on donkey, mule, horse, or carried by villager. Extra money comes to women to shop. Rumshops livelier with men. Everybody gets a little share. Now — requirements change. Competition fiercer. Better quality fruit is demanded. Small-man grower sells locally. Only big planters can manage it fo' overseas market.'

Boy-Don was surprised. He thought banana-growing had always been the same. His thinking flashed on to how Mr Burke's field of bananas near his home was given all kind of special, special care. Hanging bunches of bananas were fattened up in a green mesh sack, like a lady's glove up her arm full length. That kept the bunch free of insect or leaf scratch. He found he somehow had a funny sort of envy for the travel and far-away life of bananas. He imagined how the bananas would travel on a ship on that big, big sea, all landless, touching the skyline all round. And the bananas would arrive in a city, like another world.

Surrounded by a foreign language, they'd get carried in gold baskets. In a strange home they'd get arranged in a bowl all gold. And some would get cooked in frying pans with gold handles. He remembered how when his brother-and-sister cousins from New York visited, he took them to their land up 'the bush' on a donkey. He took them coconut and mango picking and sea bathing. He took them to the banana packing-house. But best of all was taking them jumping the irrigation ditches – playing a game of crisscrossing in the air – in Mr Burke's banana field ... He said, 'And so, banana-day different now, sir?'

'One thing not changed, Boy-Don.'

'What's that?'

'Waiting at the wharf to get unloaded on to the ship.'

'You have to wait while the ship's waiting?'

'Long line of trucks will be there before me, loading on.'

The docked ship and the bananas being loaded on made Boy-Don think. He was glad Mr Burke went quiet. Then he began watching how Mr Burke drove the truck. Going round corners Mr Burke pressed the horn on and on like a machine giving money, making a great ten-trumpets fanfare noise. The mountain of a load made the engine moan up-hill and, like a welcome relief, changed downhill to a sound all relaxed. Mr Burke drove through villages blowing his horn, making pigs, goats, dogs or fowl scuttle off out of the way for dear life. When Mr Burke rested longest on his full-blast ten-trumpets horn, they had stopped four miles from the town, at Granny-May's house. And there was Granny-May and Miss Gee hurrying down towards the closed white gate.

Dressed differently in their own neat home-made summer frocks, Miss Gee's dress had leaf patterns while Granny-May's was plain white, with a stack of thin coloured bracelets on her wrists. Though Miss Gee was older, the tall and slim sisters looked similar, smiling together as they came to the gate.

Looking down from her tall height, Granny-May said, 'Nicholas! Boy! What a way you've got big, and beautiful! Let me hug you and kiss you.' But while she hugged and kissed Boy-Don he felt surprised, sad and disappointed that Granny-May called him Nicholas. Nowadays nobody called him Nicholas. And Miss Gee went through all the hugging and kissing too, adding more. Boy-Don felt helpless and shocked at how everybody knew his new name except them.

The way his new name had come to him was like a real miracle. Clear-clear, it all came back in his head . . .

That day at school – a really vile and vicious day! He'd come home fed up, looking terrible, nothing but misery. He knew he had the silliest, stupidest name in the whole world. His name was worries! Everywhere – in whispers in class, in shouts on school playground, on the road going home – 'Knickers!' 'Knickers!' 'Want a game, Knickers?' Or the stupid, 'Hi there, Nick-The-Nicker-To-Be-Nicked-For-Nicking!' 'How's Nick-The-Nicker?' 'Nick-The-Knickers, hi there!'

Oh, it was bad. Feeling all terrible and fed up, he'd sat on the back veranda. Hannah had come and sat on the bench. 'I have the worst-worst name in the world,' he'd said.

'What you mean?'

'I just mean I have the stupidest name.'

'Nicholas is a great brilliant name.'

'Nicholas, Nick, Knickers — I hate it!'

'Wait. Wait here a minute.' Hannah got up, went, came back with the encyclopedia and read from it. Hannah first explained that because his birthday was December 6th their parents honoured his birthday by naming him after Saint Nicholas. She read how Saint Nicholas' life was full of giving gifts and doing good deeds. And Saint Nicholas was so important that his saintly feast-day celebration was changed from December 6th that it could be kept up on Christmas Day.

'But nobody at school knows anything about all that!' he'd said crossly.

'That's because they're ignorant and stupid.'

'Then why even you have to read it from a book? And not just tell me out of your head?'

'Because I want to show you it's true.'

'Well I don't believe. And nobody at school would believe.'

'Then you should explain how important your name is.'

'Have you ever been laughed at by everybody? Eh? Have you ever been laughed at?'

'Of course I have.'

'I have an idea.' He'd said that quietly, holding his head down.

'What idea?' Hannah said doubtfully.

'You know our dad's name is Mr Donald Wallman?'

'Of course I know that.'

'So – he's big man Don.'

'What you getting at?'

He'd jumped up and shouted. 'Our dad's Big-Don! I am Boy-Don! Boy-Don's my real name. That's my name – Boy-Don!'

'Ahh! Stupid!' His sister had sneered. 'And, who, who's going to take the slightest bit of notice of any "Boy-Don"?'

'I'm doing some rap rhymes to go with it.'

'Some what?'

'Rap rhymes.'

'What's that?'

'You know rapping! Anyway, you'll see. And I have something special to go with it. I have a special cap-wearing style to go with my rap rhymes ...'

And, boy, the whole thing worked like the magic of iced lemonade! Everybody wanted it. All the girls and boys wanted him over and over to perform his rap rhymes. Everybody wanted to see his style of dance with his rap sound going –

> I'm the boy called Boy-Don
> well known as number one style man ...
> the way me one wear my cap
> with my style of rap ...

It went on in school playground. On school road it went on. 'Boy-Don! Boy-Don!' the girls and boys shouted. 'Perform "Boy Called Boy-Don"!' 'Perform

"Boy-Don"!' 'Do "Mighty Frog"!' 'Yes, do "Mighty Frog"!' 'No, no. Do "Long Face, Hee-aw ..."!' They shouted, 'Do it again! Again! Again!' Twice, up at village square, Saturday evenings, he did 'Mighty Frog' over and over. Cap turned sideways, arms swinging in rhythm, head nodding —

> In the lane at my trot of a jog
> I met the one Mighty Frog.
> I looked him up
> he looked me up.
> I looked him down
> he looked me down.
> Then I said, 'Hello, bush folk.'
> Then he said, 'GROAK GROAK.'
>
> I jumped round, 'Hello, bush folk.'
> He jumped round, 'GROAK GROAK.
>   GROAK GROAK.'
> We danced in bright moonlight,
> danced round on till daylight.
> Boy-Don — 'Hello, bush folk,'
> Mighty Frog — 'GROAK GROAK. GROAK
>   GROAK.'
>
> Mighty Frog disappeared
> and Boy-Don disappeared —
> 'Hello, bush folk.'
> 'GROAK GROAK. GROAK GROAK ...'

It went on and on, with the girls and boys joined in jumping round, 'GROAK GROAK. GROAK GROAK ...'

This new name 'Boy-Don' caught on! It became the new fashion to say 'Boy-Don', 'Boy-Don', till now. Till now ...!

Granny-May gave Mr Burke a basket of things, saying it was just a few special mangoes, a melon, a pineapple and some oranges. Mr Burke drove off in his noisy horn-blowing and all three of them waved to him.

Granny-May and Miss Gee's house was clean, neat and cool. They had an electric fan in the sitting-room ceiling. They took Boy-Don into a room with a single bed. He put his bag down and came out into the backyard that had lots of Joseph-coat crotons, masses of flowers blooming, lots of vegetables planted, and spaced-out trees. Miss Gee called him back on to the back veranda. Everybody sat down and had iced lemonade. 'Nicholas, you forgot to take your cap off,' Granny-May said.

Boy-Don grabbed his cap, 'Sorry, mam.' He tucked it in beside himself in the chair.

'And d'you always wear your cap with the peak sideways, Nicholas?' Miss Gee asked.

'Not always, mam.'

'So it is deliberate?'

'Sometimes, mam.'

'Let's take him and show him the gardens,' Granny-May said.

The sisters were proud of their many flowers, vegetables and fruit trees. Boy-Don noticed the low, dwarfed coconut palm trees bearing clusters of young coconuts. The trees were so low a tall girl or boy could reach up and pick a nut.

'Would you like a water-coconut?' Granny-May asked.

'Yes, mam, I would.'

And looking up, the tall Granny-May held and twisted a green young coconut till its stem broke. She chopped off the top and Boy-Don drank the coconut-water. He heaved a sigh of pleasure, grinned and said, 'Can I have the meat, mam?'

'With a little local wet-sugar?'

'Oh, yes, yes!'

Granny-May had hardly chopped the nut open on the ground to expose its soft white jelly when Miss Gee came back with the sugar and a spoon. The wet-sugar ran like a syrup over the jelly coconut. Boy-Don scooped and ate it all up greedily while the two ladies watched.

Boy-Don rushed here and there in the yard. He held on to the fence of the chicken-run, looking at the fowls inside it, and unexpectedly felt he'd seen everything. He looked round and saw Granny-May and Miss Gee doing little jobs in their gardens. Somewhere in his tummy Boy-Don felt a loneliness like a first day at school. He watched the rooster and hens in the chicken-run, for a bit. He walked slowly up to his Granny. 'Granny-May, can we go to the sea?'

'Oh, yes, yes, Nicholas. I was going to suggest it. Let's go now.'

They had a short walk along the main road. In both directions in the distance, noisy horn-blowing of the unseen banana-trucks came to them. Granny-May and

Boy-Don turned on to a lane of very tall coconut palm trees. Suddenly, an endless sea opened out before them, under endless sky.

Only two couples could be seen on the warm and bright white sand beach. Sunlight poured down. The clear space of wide, wide sea was wonderful. Boy-Don threw himself down on the sand. He shoved his hands down into the loose hot sand and let it run freely through his fingers. He wrenched his feet out of his sneakers. He looked down at the busy water around his legs. The waves rolled out on to the sand and rushed back.

'Granny-May? Take off your shoes and come in.'

'I doubt that, Nicholas.'

'Did you bring my swim trunks, mam?'

'Did you bring them with you in your bag from home?'

'I don't think so, mam.' And Boy-Don rushed out of the water. He tore off his denim trousers and shirt and dropped them on the sandbank. In his little white briefs he hopped and threw himself chest down flat into the sea and began swimming about.

Granny-May stood at the edge of the water and watched her grandson enjoying himself like a lively little dolphin. He dived down and she stood with drawn breath till he surfaced again. He waited for a biggish wave, jumped over it like a dog over an obstacle and she smiled. He waited for another wave, deliberately let it wash over him and she looked worried. He swam backwards and let the waves dump him on the sand and she was thrilled at how well her grandson swam and controlled his little body in the sea. And Boy-Don enjoyed feeling the big sea shoving him about without something there for him to bounce against. Again and again he played that game. But unexpectedly, once more he wanted company. He was used to having brothers in the sea with him. He missed them. Big Andy always gave him a swim out on his back. Or they all played at fighting off sharks in a lot of terror noise, or splashed each other crazily. Or they jumped waves together. Boy-Don felt enough was enough on his own in the water. He came out of the sea wanting to lie down on the sand and not talk. But Granny-May was all over him, drying him down with a towel and going on about what a wonderful swimmer he was.

'Andy and Hannah are both better'n me, mam.'

'Better swimmers?'

'Yes. Much, much! They'll swim out to our beach rock in the sea and jump down into the deep water. I can't do that.'

'I should hope not. That must be dangerous. Must be.'

'Only one thing though, mam, I can do better than all of them.'

'So what's that?'

'I'm best at drawing and making rhymes.'

'Drawing and making rhymes?'

'Yes, mam.'

'That's two things. You're not good at arithmetic, Nicholas.'

Boy-Don smiled. 'No, mam. That's my worst subject.'

'And I found you out!'

Boy-Don grinned wider. 'Yes, mam.'

'So what d'you draw? And what d'you make rhymes about?'

'Oh, mam, I draw big, bad, ugly dogs with terrible fangs and claws and eyes of fire. And, mam, they're sneaky dogs. Really sneaky!'

'Why bad, ugly dogs? Why not nice dogs?'

'I already have a nice dog.'

'Well, why not draw a donkey or a cow?'

'A donkey is a beast of burden. A donkey doesn't keep watch. A donkey doesn't have the chance to be bad like a dog.'

'And a cow?'

'A cow can't be a friend or a terrible enemy like a dog.'

'So, I can see, Nicholas, you do think a lot about it all.'

'No, mam. I only draw pictures with a feeling. It's now when you question me I find I have an answer.'

'So what about the rhymes you make?'

'My rhymes are about a silly story. You'd find them really silly.'

'Did you bring one to show me?'

'Bring one, mam?' For a little bit Boy-Don was confused. Rap rhymes had rushed into his head —

> In the lane at my trot of a jog
> I met the one Mighty Frog.
> I looked him up

he looked me up.
I looked him down
he looked me down ...

'Yes. Did you bring one to show me?'

'No, mam. Nothing written down. But you wouldn't like it anyway. You wouldn't like it. You wouldn't.' But the lines kept repeating in his head — 'In the lane at my trot of a jog, I met the one Mighty Frog ...'

He knew it all by heart. He wished, wished, he could right there perform this rap rhyme. But it was too silly. He couldn't, couldn't do it. If it was from a book he'd recite it. But he made it all up himself.

'Next time will you bring me one of your rhymes and show me?'

Boy-Don was still doubtful. 'Well, mam — I tell you what, I'll ask Andy. If Andy says it's okay, it'll be okay. It'll be fine.'

'You're nice and dry now. Except for your wet underpants. Why not take them off and put your other things on.'

Granny-May was sitting on the sandbank, shaded by her broad straw hat with patterns of red roses on it. She took off her sun-glasses and looked out over the sea. And Granny-May seemed full of dreams.

'I'll soon be back, mam.'

Granny-May looked at Boy-Don and smiled.

Boy-Don breezed off, running, kicking up sand along the beach. He stopped, threw himself down and looked around him. He dug down hard with both hands, scooping up sand. His digging had the exact rhythm of his 'Frog' rap rhymes. Nobody hearing him, Boy-Don performed 'Mighty Frog' to his sand-digging and the sound of the sea.

> In the lane at my trot of a jog
> I met the one Mighty Frog ...
> ... Boy-Don — 'Hello bush folk,'
> Mighty Frog — 'GROAK, GROAK GROAK GROAK.' ...

Afterwards, Boy-Don walked back along the beach, looking for any special thing the sea might have dumped. He looked up and there was Granny-May walking towards him.

'Look, Granny-May! Look what I found!'

'Root of a little tree. Could make an ornament.'

'Yes, mam. Polished up a bit more than the job sea and sand done already. It's a guava tree root. Best it could make a small gig.'

'A top.'

'Yes, mam.'

'I'll put it in my bag. And the others? What's the others?'

Boy-Don held up a few shells, a big red back of a crab and a small and slender piece of sea-polished timber. Granny popped the things in her bag and said, 'We'd better be going. Miss Gee will have lunch ready and waiting.' They sat down on the beach-hut bench. Granny-May wiped and brushed sand from his feet and between his toes. She put on his sneakers and laced them up. All this looking-after made Boy-Don cringe.

He hated it. Did Granny think he was a baby? Eh? Could Granny ever know he was the real big Boy-Don?

At the house Miss Gee had a fresh white cloth on a table laid for lunch on the back veranda. The big mango tree shaded the veranda from afternoon sun.

Boy-Don cooled his thirst with iced lemonade straightaway. And, boy, was he hungry! 'Fresh Fish Run-Down' was just what he wanted. The fish with chopped spring onions, garlic, tomatoes, pepper and other seasoning had been added to coconut milk boiled to a curdle. Simmered with everything to a reddened rich gravy sauce, the 'Run-Down' looked terrific. Served with yams, boiled green bananas, dumplings, okra and spinach-like calaloo, the fish meal went down like best food at a feast. Then the skinned ripe bananas baked with butter, brown sugar and nutmeg, ended a meal when parts of a boy still wanted to carry on.

Lunch over, Boy-Don drifted round the backyard. He passed the beds of flowers and the vegetable garden mixed with small coconut trees. Walking on, he saw that the place was an enormous land compared to his own backyard. Orange and grapefruit trees were here. Breadfruit and mango trees. Nutmeg and pimento-berry trees. Tall and skyward coconut trees. A cluster of sugar-cane. Banana, plantain, coffee trees. All sorts of trees were spaced out here. Almost every tree was bearing fruit, or was in blossom. Wondering, looking, thinking, Boy-Don heard Granny-May's voice break through, calling him. He turned round, answered and ran back to the house.

In their sitting-room, under the spinning fan of the ceiling, the two sisters were comfortably seated. Granny-May told Boy-Don this was no time of day to be out in the sun. She made him sit down on the sofa. She told him to stay there and rest himself. The cat came in and snuggled herself up at the other end of his sofa. Miss Gee asked Boy-Don questions about how he was getting on at school. He answered Miss Gee in ways it seemed to him he might please her. And that seemed to work. Miss Gee used to be a music teacher. She told Boy-Don she'd play the organ for him later. Then, except for the fan, the place went quiet.

Boy-Don began to think how much he'd like to draw. He remembered he had nothing to draw with. Then, he noticed, Granny-May and Miss Gee were asleep! Fast asleep! All this was odd, really odd, Boy-Don thought. The sisters fell asleep like this every afternoon, but Boy-Don didn't know. He kept looking at the two ladies, wondering if they were dead. They weren't really dead. But they were odd. And he couldn't go away. Granny-May put him to sit there on the sofa. If only he could do something. But he couldn't draw, couldn't think up rap rhymes, couldn't play with his dog Browndash or Rhino or Goaty. He couldn't talk, couldn't perform to his brothers and sister. And — a week! Here for a week! A whole, whole week! Loneliness, that sad loneliness of a first day at school, came again and was heavy in Boy-Don's tummy. The whole inside of the room, the buzz of the spinning fan, the quiet curtains, the quiet tables and chairs, all was unfriendly. He sat up to pick up the cat. He'd almost touched the lovely black-and-white cat when she leapt up and rushed out of the room.

It was all such a silly, stupid baby thing to do. Yet here he was crying. Boy-Don was crying. He kept thinking of Browndash, Goaty and Rhino. But he didn't stop crying.

Granny-May and Miss Gee slept till the sun moved and it was cooler. He tried to conceal he'd been crying but couldn't. He just could not explain why he had become so sad and tears kept streaming down his face. He could only say, 'I don't know. I don't know why I cry. I don't want to cry. But here I am crying.'

The two sisters were really surprised and concerned. Miss Gee said, 'Shall I play the organ for you? Would you like that?'

'I don't think it'll help, mam.'

'Shall I sing some children's songs for you?'

'They make me think of other things, mam.'

'Shall I tell you a story?'

'Yes — if it's about bad dogs.'

'Well — can't say I know any of those.'

Granny-May said, 'Would you like a glass of lemonade?'

'Yes, thanks, mam.' Boy-Don drank, and the tears continued to come.

Granny-May went on. 'Would you like us to go for a walk round the yard land at the back?'

'We can try.'

All the walking around the land and the pointing out of different trees and birds in them did not stop Boy-Don's crying.

'You'll have to pull yourself together, Nicholas. You're here for a week. You'll have to give yourself a chance. You wake up in the morning and you'll see it's all different. You'll be your bright self again.'

Tears gushed down Boy-Don's face more quickly. He wished, wished, Granny-May would stop trying to find a way to make him want to stay. He couldn't say it himself that staying was like staying in a tomb. He couldn't admit just thinking of going to bed one night here made him want to die. To die! He wanted, wanted, the voices, noises, smells, everybody, everything and all the goings on at his house, so much that it hurt. It hurt badly, badly.

Granny-May held her handkerchief to his nose and asked him to blow. Then she wiped his face. 'Can't you tell me how you really feel?'

'I can't, mam. I really can't. I don't know is nearest answer.'

'D'you feel ill?'

'No, mam. Not really. Crying like this I just feel silly and stupid and bad, mam. But I can't stop myself.'

Looking at him, Granny-May went on. 'Nicholas, you know you'll have to stop crying, don't you?'

'All the time I'm trying.'

'Well, you're here for a week. We're going to have a nice, nice time. I have plans made for us.'

Boy-Don looked away. Tears came down in a new and stronger stream. 'Plans made for us' — whatever,

whatever they were — it frightened him, it hurt him. That odd belly pain took away his strength. It put a hold on him and made him helpless. It made him know he'd be carried off away into loneliness and loneliness. Boy-Don sobbed. He really felt foolish. He didn't know he could feel such a lost, lost boy and such a baby.

Granny-May was cross. She was concerned. She was worried. But, mostly, she was sad Nicholas was so unhappy. She stooped down. Face to face, she took Boy-Don's sobbing face into her hands lovingly and said, 'Nicholas, Nicholas, you are with Granny-May. You are here with me. You will feel better. We're going to have a nice, nice time.'

'We should, mam. We should. And I'm spoiling it.'

'Never mind. You'll soon feel better. You'll see.'

'My eyes must be red, mam. My eyes red?'

'I'm afraid your eyes are red. They've been flooded on and on for some time now! But never mind.' She hugged him, kissed him and wiped his face again. 'Never mind. You'll feel better tomorrow.'

That word 'tomorrow' was a terror rather than a comfort to Boy-Don! He couldn't stay till tomorrow! The word was like a sentence for him to be locked away in prison. Tears came down freely. He looked up at his granny with his wet, tear-sodden face, 'How you going to stop me crying, mam? How you going to stop me?'

His granny certainly didn't say, I'll see that you get back home tonight. She said, 'We go back and play cricket. Would you like to play cricket?'

And he answered, 'We can try, mam. We can go and try.'

'Come on.'

The sun had been going away gradually. Tree shadows were longer now. At the house Granny-May brought out a rubber ball with her dead husband's cricket bat and wickets. She began bowling underarm to Boy-Don's batting. His tears came with sobbing. They had to give up the game with Granny-May saying, 'Nicholas, you'll have to stop this crying. You'll have to stop it! Otherwise I'll just have to put you to bed and lock you up early, by yourself.'

Granny-May's threats held out and stuck to a nothing else but a stay for the night, and perhaps longer. His awful pain got worse. His tummy was heavy and strange and made him weak. It was very, very sad how he felt alone and lost in a strange wild place and there was no way ever to get home again.

Washed in tears, full of apologies, eating at the table in the dining-room with Granny-May and Miss Gee, Boy-Don felt helpless. Then, a truck stopped down at the gate. Its ten-trumpets fanfare horn was sounded! Going home with empty truck from his last trip it was Mr Burke coming up to the front veranda.

'Just a friendly stop,' he said, 'to see if Boy-Don would like me to take a message home for him.'

'A message? A message?' Tears vanished, Boy-Don said, looking round at everybody on the veranda now. 'Can I go? Can I go back with Mr Burke? His truck is empty, mam. All empty! Mr Burke, sir, can I come back with you? Granny-May, can I go?'

Granny-May's disappointment was swallowed in silence before she said, 'How will you explain your short, short stay with us?'

'I won't, mam. I won't. And everybody will know it's my fault.' Tears gone, Boy-Don was wide-eyed, pleading with his granny.

'Get your bag. Next time, I will come and stay with you.'

'Yes, mam. Yes, mam. Do that. Me, Browndash, Goaty and Rhino will take you out walking.'

The big glow of orange sun was sinking behind the sea when Boy-Don arrived home. Astounded, unable to believe that he'd actually come back home on the first evening, everybody came quickly on to the veranda and stood speechless. Bag hanging from his shoulder, cap on his head turned sideways, Boy-Don shoved Granny-May's quickly written letter into his mother's hand and disappeared.

'Boy-Don, come back here!' Mrs Wallman demanded. 'Come right back here and tell what happened!'

Boy-Don came out again. He busily searched in one pocket after the next, as if he had much, much more important matters to deal with. 'Mama,' he said, 'please can I go and do something very, very urgent? And first I must change my clothes.'

'Stay right here and talk! You went off to Granny-May for one week. Why have you come back first night?'

Boy-Don was quick and confident. 'All's in the letter, mam. All's in the letter.'

'Mister Bigshot couldn't bear spending even one night away from home,' Hannah said, 'let alone a week.'

'I'm dying to know what happened,' eight-year-old Mark said. And he joined his tickled sister, not able to stop tittering.

'The brief note only says, "Nicholas had a severe attack of homesickness,"' their mum said. 'And, "a longer letter will follow."'

'Homesickness!' Hannah screamed. Mark rolled about in fits.

'Boy-Don,' Mark said, 'did you vomit?'

The children screamed out laughing before their mum could say, 'Stop it! Stop it!'

'After all that elaborate preparation – and fuss – to get away,' Hannah said. 'Didn't I say you'd have nothing interesting to say when you got back? Didn't I?' Hannah couldn't stop herself laughing. 'Didn't I, Boy-Don? Eh? Answer me.'

Mark said, 'I wish I'd been invited, don't you, Hannah?'

'I bet you,' Hannah said, 'I bet you he cried. Did you cry at Granny-May's, Boy-Don? Did you start crying?'

Boy-Don only gave Hannah a bitter glaring look.

'Come on now,' their dad Headmaster Mr Wallman said, 'give him a break. He'll talk when he's ready. You will, won't you, Boy-Don?'

'Yes, Dad.'

'Then, come closer. And say what happened.'

Boy-Don went and stood beside his dad. 'Well, sir – at first, it was exciting. Then – then, it wasn't.'

'Why wasn't it exciting any more?'

'Well – Granny-May and Miss Gee went to sleep. Fast asleep.'

Hannah screamed, 'Went to sleep? And left you?'

'Yes. Went to sleep. And had me in the room to go to sleep as well. And I couldn't sleep. And I couldn't leave the room. I didn't want to disobey.'

A situation like this had not been considered. Everybody now listened keenly to Boy-Don.

The fascinated Hannah said, 'For how long? How long did they put you to bed for?'

Mark couldn't hold back his giggle. But Boy-Don took no notice. 'I was in the room watching them sleep for a long, long time.'

'And what happened?'

'It was like Granny-May and Miss Gee were dead – or dying all the time. And I was left all alone. And I missed everybody. I missed everybody at home so, so much. And it was like I known everybody here a long long time ago. And I wouldn't find you again. And it was sad, sad!'

'And did you cry?'

'Dad, please will you ask my sister not to bother me?'

'Sister, don't bother your brother. And – so – you came back home, first night?'

'Dad, I couldn't bear not coming back – this very, very night.'

'Well – you're back home.'

Boy-Don didn't dare look at his dad. A terrible weight had been lifted off him. He felt all a new man again. And he said, 'Thank you, Daddy. Thank you, sir.' And Boy-Don disappeared as swiftly as he could, with Browndash behind him. He went to see Goaty, in a little outhouse in the backyard. Goaty was lying down chewing her cud. Still chewing, happy to see him, she looked at him, then looked away and listened to his voice. Boy-Don stroked his goat, saying all about how he was back. Then he and his dog rushed off again. At the pigpen, Rhino also was lying down. Happy to see Boy-Don, the pig grunted specially. Boy-Don stroked Rhino, telling him all about how he was home again. Then, in the dusk of the thickening night, Boy-Don and Browndash ran round and round the yard, playing.

Boy-Don felt he was outside of the family right now. He knew everybody was cross with him. He stayed away from talking to anybody.

Lights had come on in the house. Except for Andy, everybody was sitting on the front veranda, getting the little cooler night breeze. Andy sat under a light in the sitting-room, reading. Boy-Don came to him and whispered, 'Andy, please, can you announce to everybody I want to perform?'

Big brother Andy held the book down. He stared straight into his little brother's face. 'You mean you want to have a go at making things up with everybody, don't you?'

'I, I didn't say that.'

'But you want to try to mend your day's bad-behaviour damage? Right?'

'I'm not saying that.'

'All the same, it's that you want to get back into

everybody's good books. Isn't it?'

'Don't say that when you announce me,' Boy-Don shook his head, staring back into Andy's face. 'Don't, don't, don't say that.'

'How much you going to pay me?'

'How much you charge?'

'I'm not cheap. D'you think I'm cheap?'

'I'm not a poor man. Do you think I'm a poor man?'

Andy chuckled and grinned. He got up, leaving his book on the table. He went straight out on to the veranda. 'Announcement! Boy-Don would like to do a performance of his rap rhymes for everybody!'

'That's a piece of cheek!' Hannah said. 'Does he think anybody's even speaking to him?'

'Hannah,' Andy said slowly, 'I am directing and presenting this show. Okay?' He looked round and saw Boy-Don standing in the doorway. At fourteen years old, Andy's voice was changing. He went for his big dramatic announcement. He threw his arms wide open and his voice was loud, 'FOR HIS FAMILY!' Andy's voice went astray. His husky voice broke into a peculiar high note. Then it came husky again and ran into strange sounds, as he said, 'OUR OWN BOY-DON PERFORMS HIS RAP RHYMES!'

Nobody could hold back. A grin or a smile on every face, everybody clapped.

The veranda lights weren't switched on. Its light was a reflection of lights from the sitting and bed rooms. Boy-Don stepped out, dancing, in the dim veranda light. Peak of cap turned sideways over his ear, arms swinging in rhythm, head nodding, he was into it.

> 'Hello,' I said to the donkey I saw
> he said, 'Boy-Don, HEE-AW,
> HEE-AW, HEE-AW, HEE-AW!'

> I saw the horse with his long face
> just by a nose won his race.

> I saw my very own Hog
> sitting there on a log
> I said, 'Hog — so you really think?'
> Hog said, 'OINK? OINK? OINK? OINK?'

Everybody clapped.

'Do it again!' Hannah yelled. 'Do it again.'

Boy-Don looked round to see if everybody agreed. 'Yes, yes!' Mr Wallman said 'Encore! Encore!'

Not only once, but twice, arms swinging, head nodding, Boy-Don had to do his 'Hee-aw, Long Face' again.

'Do "The Mongoose",' Andy said.

'The Mongoose?' Hannah said.

'Yes,' Andy said. 'About the mongoose who comes to the fence — '

'And makes a noise,' Hannah chipped in, 'to get fowls confused so he can catch them!'

'As it is said by folk wisdom.'

Hannah insisted. 'We've all heard them at the fence or a little way off under cover, doing their terrible shrill cry.'

'Boy-Don?' Andy said. 'You were working on your

"Mongoose" rap rhymes. Was it finished?'

'Long time.'

'You'd like to do it?'

Arms swinging in rhythm, head nodding, Boy-Don was at it again.

> Listen to the mongoose
> calling fowls out of henhouse
>
> SHRISH-SHRISH-SHRISH,
> SHRISH-SHRISH-SHRISH
> you are sweeter than fish
> come on let me eat you up
> come on be my sweet sup-sup!
>
> Listen to the mongoose
> calling fowls out of henhouse
>
> SHRISH-SHRISH-SHRISH,
> SHRISH-SHRISH-SHRISH
> you are sweeter than fish
> come on let me eat you up
> come on be my sweet sup-sup!

'Again! Again!' Boy-Don heard and performed his 'Mongoose' rap rhymes three times.

His dad embraced him. His mum embraced him. Hannah embraced him. Andy and Mark didn't embrace him. But he knew, Boy-Don well knew, everything was all right again at home with everybody.

Son-Son Fetches the Mule

Animals have another sense, it would seem. They know when you are a child, and they love you for being a child. An animal will let a child pet him, boss him and even handle him upside-down, in any crazy or awkward old way, like he was dead. He would love it and give himself up to it, limply and totally. But there are other times when an animal hates it if a boy gets the better of him. That happened to Son-Son. Just fetching the mule, Son-Son found himself in trouble with him. Not expecting it, the good-good behaviour of the work mule was all spite, all vicious teeth and hooves kicked up in the air. And now Son-Son had the mule to fetch as a regular morning job, before school.

Yesterday — first time he started this new job — the mule gave him a really bad time. He played bad man. Could have damaged him! And nobody must ever know — *must ever know* — he couldn't handle Maroon-tugger, couldn't deal with him. Son-Son knew it and saw it: this job was his job. He must do it by himself.

Like yesterday, today was an everyday warm tropical early morning. Son-Son carried a coil of rope over his shoulder. His dad had told him to carry it. He should use the rope to make a halter around Maroon-tugger's head, before he untethered him.

Son-Son came alone into the field of high grass.

Much more excited than worried, he felt good. And he looked good. He wore his long peaked white cap, short-sleeved floral shirt, short trousers and his sandals. He walked under one of the coconut-palm trees that stood scattered about. Even when his sandals and toes quickly got wet with dew from the grass and weeds he didn't mind. Son-Son took no notice of the morning sunlight or the tree shadows. He took no notice of noisy birds fluttering in trees, doing peep-peeps, squawk-squawks, coo-coos or just straight singing. Son-Son's job made him walk nippily on, eyes ahead. Everything about him made him look purposeful.

In truth, Son-Son was thinking he liked the business of helping his dad. It made him feel grown-up. But, best, really, it was great to handle and ride the big mule totally on his own. He'd handled Maroontugger before, lots of times, though not by himself, till yesterday. They knew each other well. Yet when he came to take Maroontugger in for work yesterday, the mule treated him like a stranger. The mule put on a bad bad face. Tried to attack him! He had to jump quick, away from the mule's kicks! And he wouldn't let him get the loop of rope round his long head; he wouldn't let him get on his back to ride him home; then he kicked-up and kicked-up, trying to throw him off.

At one time yesterday he'd got worried his job was taking him too long. And he'd figured it out that the mule didn't at all like a ten-year-old taking him in for work. Then he'd also seen that it wasn't anything about *him* that Maroontugger disliked. The mule worked too hard. And, after all, who could blame him trying to get a day off? But a job was a job. He had to show Maroontugger that he had a job to do, just as he, Son-Son, had a job to do as well. And bad and vicious as the mule was, he had to take him in for work.

Son-Son came on into the field lit with morning sunlight. He saw Maroontugger. He was still feeding — head down in the field of high grass and scattered trees. Son-Son stopped. He watched the mule. He saw Maroontugger and yesterday's terrible mule-madness went from him. Evaporated! Son-Son felt good. It was great to be there alone with this big elephant-looking reddish fellow. He listened to the mule's greedy and noisy chewing. The huge jaws with half-circles of axe-like grabber teeth chewed grass again and again. The working of the big jaws made a noise like a grinding in an empty barrel. Son-Son's eyes widened and shone. 'Jees!' he thought. 'Terrific! Terrific how the grinding of the strong and loud eating has no good manners! No good manners at all!'

In his friendliest voice, Son-Son said, 'Good mornin', Maroontug! Good mornin'!'

The mule lifted his head, tossed his long ears forward and stopped chewing. His steady eyes watched Son-Son. And Son-Son couldn't guess that in the straight look the mule said, 'Oh! So that's it! It's you again. The boss sent you again. You the boy to take me in for work! Well, we'll see! We'll see about that, won't we?'

Son-Son grinned. 'Ahright, Maroontugger? Between we, you an' me the tops, you know! Ahright?' The mule's long ears, tossed forward over his eyes, reminded him of his own long peaked cap on his head.

He walked forward. 'Had a good night, Tugger-boy? Sleeping alone under stars?' Son-Son stopped again, looking round, fascinated as he had been the morning before. The high grass had been eaten or trampled down in a circle, as much as the mule's rope would allow. Son-Son said, 'So you eat an' eat all through the night! No sleep, then? You just eat an' eat right through till daylight? Gosh! I couldn't do that. I couldn't eat all night like that, Tugger-boy.' He looked at the mule's huge bulge of two-sided belly. 'Look at your belly! Jees! Look at you! I bet you the greediest an' strongest mule, ever. I bet you could pull away any great-house. And could run away pulling any bus-load of people! Or any high-up loaded banana-truck! Listen, listen, Maroontug! I just get a great new idea.

'Everyday's always so, so sunny an' hot. Suppose, one day – one day – when it really raining hard, I take you fo' a wet gallop, an' you take me fo' the wet-wet ride? Eh? How about that? Roun' an' roun' the big pasture land fo' a good wet rainy gallop, when the two of we soak-soak to the skin, dripping? Eh? Naw? Dohn like it? Okay. I think again.

'You always working. An' I always going school. Suppose, one day – one day – I dohn go school an' you dohn go work, an' we just team up? We team up big-big. We go cricket match. You walk beside me. We walk like man an' man. No rope on your head or anything. An' then, we stand together an' watch play-ball. Just watch! An' I explain the whole game to you. Then, then, when I have my best-best favourite thing – which is my barbeque jerk pork an' dry bread – I get

you some sugar. Naw? No good? Well — when I have
my second best-best favourite thing — which is fried
fish and fried dumplin', followed by cool, ginger beer —
I get you a pint-a stout. Naw? I can see you would-a
like rum. Noh. No rum. I cahn buy rum like that. But —
all the same — Maroontug, I got to go school. An' you
got-to go work. An' I must take you in. So, I better.'

The mule stood there all the time, staring. Son-Son
walked up to him, taking the coil of rope from his
shoulder. He reached up to put the rope round its head
and the mule's rebellion again was on. The meanest,
wildest attacking look came over the mule's face. It
flattened its ears back against its head. A swift dread
in Son-Son's face said, stop it! stop it! as the mule
swung round and kicked out at Son-Son. Only swift
evasive movement saved him. But mud from the mule's
iron shoes had flown up to his cheek and stuck. The
mule trotted off, turned its back and stood at the full
stretch of its rope, looking away.

Really cross, Son-Son was brisk. Wiping the soft
blob of earth and grass from his cheek, he rushed up
to the mule's face and shouted. 'Maroontugger! What
you think you playing at? Eh? What you think you
doing? You think you all wild, stupid, bad and fool-
fool! Why you behaving like you have no training?
An' no respect? You want a good friend get rough an'
careless with you? You wahn me beat you? You wahn
feel my whip hand? I tell you — dohn change me. You
well know, you a good trained worker. An' I Son-Son,'
tapping his chest with his fingers, 'I the man who must
take you in. Take you in fo' work. This very mornin'.

Understan'? Ahright? So no more wild foolishness! You hear me? Good. I going put the rope round your head, softly, softly. Know that. So, easy now. Easy ... Steady now, boy ... Steady. Easy now ...'

As Son-Son again was about to slip the wide loop of rope over Maroontugger's head, the mule bared his enormous teeth and clapped his jaws together near Son-Son's face. Horror-struck, 'Stop et!' he bawled. His screaming rage echoed through the field and panicked the mule. It tossed its head in the air, backed off, turned round and walked away. Again it stood with its rear end turned on Son-Son, as if to say, 'Go away. I don't want to see you. Don'y want anybody collecting me. Don't want any work. Sweating, sweating, all day, pulling logs uphill, pulling, pulling ...'

Son-Son felt upset and looked it. It hurt him that Maroontugger didn't take him as a friend. 'How can he not take me as a friend?' he whispered. He looked out up and down along the track at the side of the land. He stood still in the grassy field. If his dad came after him there'd be trouble. His dad knew he'd handled Maroontugger before. He might forget it was never by himself — except yesterday. It would be hard to make his dad believe Maroontugger wanted to hurt or scare him off. And — he had other morning jobs to do.

Unexpectedly, Son-Son felt better. He knew — he just knew — it wasn't himself Maroontugger disliked. For sure, it was hard work the mule wanted a rest from. True-true, the mule's job was sweaty, terrible. Two other mules tugged and pulled timber logs up to the sawmill with Maroontugger. Even so, cutting up the hillside was neither fun nor easy game to play. And whether his dad worked Maroontugger himself or not, the mule went uphill-downhill, all day long in the hot-hot sun.

His dad never took things easy himself. His dad gave way to nothing. His dad worked himself as hard as he worked his mule. Partner to another man using the electric saw, he ripped and ripped massive tree trunks into timber. By himself with a hand-saw, axe or machete, he cut and chopped away the tree limbs and branches. He cleared away branches and heaved logs. At sundown when he and Maroontugger came home each night, his dad's clothes were full of hot-sun smell and sweat and woodsap. And when he changed clothes, sawdust fell off his shirt and out of his turnups and boots.

Son-Son began to imagine everbody else getting on with their morning jobs at his yard. He imagined his mum at the paraffin stove getting breakfast. His oldest brother had fed the chickens and now fed the pigs. His sister tidied the house. His smaller brother had got the barrel more than half full with water from the standing-pipe on the village road. His dad had milked the cow. His dad would soon be sitting on the back steps sharpening his axe and machete. First to have breakfast, his dad could be having it any time now, giving half of it to the dog, Judoboy. All that meant he'd soon be ready to saddle up Maroontugger. He would soon want to wrap and sheath his machete and axe and then fasten them against the saddle, before he rode out of the yard with Judoboy following.

Unexpectedly, Son-Son heard a voice. 'Havin' a spot a trouble, Son-Son, mi boy?'

Son-Son swung his head round quickly and saw Mister G. He was a short man in straw hat, short sleeves and sandals, carrying a bag round his shoulder and a machete in his hand. On his way to his plot of land, Mister G had come down the lane.

'Maroontugger trying play bad-man with me, sir.'

Mister G chuckled. 'Yeh, I see that.' He stood. He and the mule looked at each other. 'Son-Son, do you job. Go right on, Son-Son. Handle him!' Mister G watched. Then he strolled away.

Son-Son began walking up to the mule. He had a new feeling. He always knew he was the mule's boss. But, now, unexpectedly, that feeling had grown much bigger. A big and bold confidence came more and more into his steps and whole body. It flowed in him like a strange magic light. The mule looked away and stood quietly, peacefully. The fearless feeling Son-Son had was terrific. He knew he had grown taller, into something almost as muscular and strong and tough as his dad. He knew this new light in him subdued the mule. He knew Maroontugger couldn't move and wouldn't move.

The mule just stood there, calm-calm, letting himself be handled. 'Tuggerboy? You see how it easy? See how it easy-easy? Nice an' easy?' Son-Son had put the big loop of rope around Maroontugger's head. He then brought it against each side of the face, all the way down to the corners of the mouth. He tied the dangling rope on one side, took it across above the nose, tied

it, drew a long loop for reins and tied it the other side
of the mule's jaw. All the time, Son-Son looked like a
midget harnessing an elephant. He completed the
halter-making, feeling good. He stroked Maroontugger's neck. 'You see is ahright. Ahright an' easy?
Eh? Ahright an' easy? Good boy.'

Son-Son led the mule to the post in the ground
where he was tethered. He loosed the rope.

Son-Son really thought his battles with Maroontugger were all over. But, Maroontugger knew differently. Maroontugger's head kept a lot more secret spite
to force Son-Son to leave him alone. As Son-Son tried
to get up on to the mule's back the new tricks started.
Every time Son-Son tried to clamber up, Maroontugger
gently eased himself away like a sideways dance. And
Son-Son came down again, right on his own two legs.
Over and over, holding on to the rope-reins against
the mule's shoulder, Son-Son heaved himself up; and
each time, that smart sideways movement made him
miss his mount and come down again. Finally, Son-
Son chuckled with a sigh, saying 'Tugger-boy – okay.
You've had your go. Now I'll have mine.'

Son-Son led the mule and tied his head close against
a coconut tree. Then, holding the end of the rope, he
climbed up the tree trunk and lowered himself down
on to the mule's back. Son-Son thought at last he'd
won; he couldn't believe the mule kept an extra reserve
store of badness saved up. The moment Son-Son drew
that slippery knot he'd tied round the tree and loosed
the mule, that was it! Maroontugger tugged his head,
swished his tail and jumped off, racing away like a wild

bull, all crazy and malicious. The mule bolted on, going its own way, without control. Son-Son could not check him. Bobbing his head with a stubborn defiance, Maroontugger raced on, going deeper into the field. He galloped recklessly under trees, trying to knock his rider off. Son-Son ducked under branches, lying down on the mule's bare back, like a North American Indian rider. His cap blew away. All the time now, he pulled and jerked and tugged at the mule's head as hard as he could, shouting, 'Whoa! Whoa! Whoa, now! Whoa, Maroontugger! Whoa, boy!'

At last, pulling and holding him firmly now, Son-Son turned Maroontugger round and held him to a walking pace. Not even allowed to break into a trot, he was ridden right back across the field out on to the track and then the village road.

Son-Son rode home into his yard on the big mule. He dismounted and tethered him, to await saddling up by his dad. The smell of brewed coffee, fried fish and breadfruit roasting on the woodfire made Son-Son realise how hungry he was.

He went into the kitchen and couldn't believe how everything was normal. And nobody said anything about taking too long fetching the mule. Nobody even mentioned he'd lost his cap. And he certainly would say nothing about it.

Nobody was ever going to say he couldn't manage Maroontugger. Nobody was even going to know the mule gave him a hard time. Yet, as he ate breakfast, Son-Son knew the struggle with Maroontugger wasn't over. But, he was ready. He was ready. Always, he was going to let that mule understand — Son-Son was tall-tall.

The Future-Telling Lady

'Neil, we almost there now,' his mother said. She sat up front beside his father, who was driving the car.

'Really great country drive, Mamma!'

'Cahn believe we never take you this way's far as this before,' his father said.

'Never. And the road-signs say we leave MoBay a hundred miles behind us. As you did say the distance was.'

'Yes. Our town Montego Bay is a bit behind us now.'

'What you going to tell Mother Eesha, Neil?'

'Me, Mamma?'

'Yeahs — you.'

Neil's face took on its fierce fighting look. 'Me wohn have anything to say to her. You and Dad brought me here.' His dad stopped the car at the side of the village road. They were beside a neatly kept hibiscus hedge, with arbours of slender flowering branches inside the yard. All the windows of the car were completely down in the warm bright Saturday morning.

'Mother Eesha may want to question you a little. Jus' to talk to you a little. Jus' for you to say something.'

Neil did not want to come for this appointment. He didn't want any going on about his 'problem'. He folded his arms and looked down. 'I'll say "Good morning, Mother Eesha." '

His father chuckled. 'Neil, you know we're only trying our best to help you.'

'Help me with what, Dad? A bit of swi-swi magic business? Beats me how you really seem to go for this sort-a thing.'

'Why d'you have this attitude, Neil?' his mother asked, in a worried but kind voice.

Neil shifted about. His face went taut. All huffy, he spat out, 'I'll tell you why. A boy at school seen Mother Eesha. Since then he's gone really stupid!'

'How has he gone stupid?'

'Brian Rowe used to come out good with Maths and some History. Since he seen Mother Eesha he's nothing but a nit!'

'Tell us why him seeing her affects you badly.'

'Mamma, cos it looks too much like swi-swi man obeah business.'

'No, no, no, Neil. Mother Eesha's nothing to do with witchcraft. Mother Eesha's a healer. Big, big difference.'

'Cahn say I like any of it.'

'What did Brian Rowe tell you?'

'He didn' tell me. I jus' hear him carrying on.'

'Saying what, Neil?'

'All about how Mother Eesha tells him about his future. All the rubbish about every name having what she calls a "name-story". Kind of message she sees in a name. Coming in a poem. And all about his future, Mamma. I dohn wahn to know about my future.'

'I'd be intrigued. All ears to know about my future.

Was his future bad, then? Wasn't it good?'

'From what Brian Rowe said, she didn' talk straight.'

'Can you remember any of what she seen in his name?'

'Lots-a nonsense about how his name gets him pestered cos he's become famous. And his name also gets him exposed, cos he's become scandalous.'

'Sounds as if he grew up and became a baddy. And gets himself in the newspaper.'

'No, mam. No. Not necessarily a baddy. It could mean jus' cos he's famous, whatever he does makes news in the papers.'

'What was the matter with Brian?' Neil's dad asked. 'What did he see Mother Eesha for?'

Neil shook his head. 'Dohn know, Dad. Never asked.'

'I think we better go in now.'

'Dad – can we wait a minute?'

'What for?'

'Might as well tell you the rest of what Brian Rowe said.'

After all his resistance, Neil was ready to talk properly. No wonder his parents looked at each other in disbelief. Without looking at his watch, his dad said. 'Yeh. Okay. We have some time.'

'Well – Brian tells us, that – without anybody telling, Mother Eesha was spot on with what he likes doing best. He said, she knew. She jus' come out with it. And she read him something from Brian's own grown-up diary. His own grown-up diary! Mam, did you know she could do that?'

'Neil, we're taking you because we know Mother Eesha helps children.'

'Yes, Neil,' his dad said, 'she's known for that.'

'I'll tell you. You see, Brian's crazy — crazy about bridges. The only other thing he does is draw aeroplanes. But tha's jus' a sideline. Always, always, he's drawing bridges. And reading about bridges. And — gets his parents to take him to see a bridge anywhere, everywhere.'

'So what did she *see* in Brian's future diary?'

Neil wanted to remember as correctly as he could. His parents didn't take their eyes off him. Right away, there, in the back of the car, his face took on the look of really hard concentration. He started slowly. 'All about — writings, about going to see bridges. Going to see — one-arch bridges to bridges with well over twenty arches. Some writing about — how, at first he merely liked bridges. Then, it was their structure in the air, over water or over a valley, that got him. And that was when he became a builder of bridges. And — some writing about — about excitement seeing a wonderful hidden-away little old bridge. Writing about — how and why a mossy one-arch wood-and-stone country bridge lasted three hundred years. Also, some writing about — standing, looking to see how a bridge fits in the landscape under the sky. And writing about — a great sensation, feeling the wood, the stone, the iron, that made a bridge. Writing about — scrambling down slopes to see the underbelly of a bridge. Seeing how a bridge stands comfortably in water, while some of it is in the air and some of it resting on the land.' Neil looked at his parents.

'That was good!' Neil's dad said. 'Really very good to remember all that.'

As if he was confused, and unsure of his feelings, Neil kept a straight face and did not smile.

'Oh, Neil!' his mother said, 'I've never heard you do anything like that so, so well! To think of remembering all that! Very, very good!'

Neil's story made his mother want to tell him something. But she wasn't sure it would help anything. She decided to stay quiet. She and Neil's dad had never told him about the unusual stories they knew about the work of Mother Eesha's mother. Mother Eesha's mother was famous for her use of herbs, her special bark and herbal baths, use of oils, and of course her healing touch.

Neil's dad and mum knew many stories about people who came to see Mother Eesha's mother for healing. And they'd been cured, when doctors had given them up as incurable. They knew stories about the dumb boy who made no sounds at all, except when Mother Eesha's mother touched him and talked to him. With her hand resting on him, the dumb boy would start singing, making the strangest of sounds. And from nowhere, dogs would arrive, gather round and howl with him as he sang. They knew stories about how a donkey would start braying when she asked it to say something. But they never tried to convince Neil of anything concerning these stories.

Mother Eesha had inherited a caring for the sick

from her mother and she had come along finding her own sympathy and skills. The community depended on her for her particular gifts and help.

'We better go in now,' Neil's dad insisted.

The car turned in and drove along the driveway. Mother Eesha's relatives lived in freshly painted bungalows on both sides of the driveway. Her land really rolled on into twenty acres. The land kept animals. And it was planted out with coconuts and bananas, with mango and other fruit trees and plots of vegetables. Usually, it wasn't only people in cars who came to see Mother Eesha. People also came on bicycles, on the backs of horses, mules and donkeys and on foot. Today was quiet.

Neil stood in the sunlight, fascinated, looking at Mother Eesha's unusual house. A neat-looking bungalow, circular, thatched, with a veranda all round, it gave Neil pleasure just to see it. While Neil was all taken up with looking, two young women came up to his parents. And – dressed in purple gowns and purple head bands – the young women took the family inside, into the reception room.

Beside everything in the room, Neil's gaze fell straightaway on two things: a large uncovered glass jar full of plain water, and a big painting of seven circles of colours, linking with each other.

Mother Eesha came in. She greeted the family, then said to Neil, 'I noticed you were looking at the painting.'

Neil's voice came out faintly. 'Yes, mam.'

Everybody looked at the painting now, as Mother

Eesha herself looked at it and explained. 'Well, it's my idea of the seven days of the week. White for Sunday, Red for Monday, Orange for Tuesday, Yellow for Wednesday, Green for Thursday, Blue for Friday, and Purple for today, Saturday. Every day, for my work, I wear my Day-Colour. As you see, today Saturday I wear my purple.'

Neil stood wide-eyed, looking at this impressive lady in her wide-sleeved purple gown and purple head-wrap. Neither tall nor short, neither black nor white, neither yellow nor red, Mother Eesha with her brown skin and her soft voice seemed like a union with everybody. Soon, swiftly, they were at the other side of the house, in a spacious open-windowed room with wickerwork furniture. The family sat with Mother Eesha round a low, glass-top circular table.

'Why the worry about Neil?' Mother Eesha asked.

'Ah, Mother Eesha!' Neil's mother said, sighing. 'Our beautiful son here steals things. He takes other children's things. And sometimes brings them home. A watch, books, pens, money, a Swiss pocket knife, a calculator — things like that! Things which often he already has! And, also, he doesn't always tell the truth. Fortunately — so far — we managed to quieten things with parents. We keep in touch with his Headmaster. But, Mother Eesha, you never know, do you, when a parent is going to be totally not approachable?'

'And punishing him doesn't seem to do much, at all,' Neil's father said.

'Mother Eesha, punishing makes him worse!'

'And our doctor doesn't have a clue as to what to do to help.'

'Goodness knows why he steals,' Neil's mother said helplessly. 'We are both honest people. We not rich. But we not poor. We can afford to buy Neil things. And we do. And he's not short of pocket money.'

'Of course this means we have to keep a sharp eye on Neil. We get him to take back everything he pinches.'

'With a letter of apology from himself and one from us.'

'Mother, you can understan', when things get to this stage, you do worry and wonder. Is he telling the truth? Is he hiding anything?'

'Which is so awful!' Neil's mother sighed again. 'All the same, Mother, I have to say, Neil and his dad do have their arguments.'

'The arguments only started when I tried to get him to take an ordinary bit of interest in sport. And I come to see he was never going to budge.'

'Ah! But is it really an ordinary bit of interest?'

'Mother Eesha, the boy's by far too small for his age. He's too twiggy. Look at him! He looks underfed. And he's not. And trying to get him to take part in anything that'll help him to put on a bit of body is like trying to get a cat to have a swim.'

'His father thinks Neil's too small for his age, but I dohn think so. I dohn think so at all. Neil's not bulky, that is so. But he's ahright. Neil's a good average for size. He's jus' not a cricket-loving, sport-loving Westindian boy! That is what he's not.'

'Does Neil do anything he himself likes doing?' Mother Eesha asked.

'That boy'll sit alone for hours and hours playing games with his computer,' his dad answered. 'He needs no company, no companion. And you'll find him awake at night, reading science fiction. The answer is, Mother Eesha, Neil's very good at playing games, indoors, alone, playing with his computer.'

Mother Eesha now kept her eyes on Neil's dad. She talked only to him for a bit. It turned out that he'd always been a big boy for his age. Also, he was a passionate cricketer, and played for a club. And, he kept up with rugger and football-playing round the world.

'So Neil is different?' Mother Eesha said to him.

'I wouldn' say it was worrying how different he was, but I'd say it makes a parent concerned.'

'So, there may be a way in Neil's nature that wants to bring something different into the family. Would you say?'

'Could be. Could be.'

'You hadn't thought of that?'

'No. No.'

Mother Eesha turned to Neil himself. 'Neil?'

'Yes, mam.'

'How d'you feel causing your parents all this worry?'

'Very bad.'

'In what way, "bad".'

'Makes me feel I wish my parents were like some other parents, mam.'

'D'you know why you cause them worry?'

'I'm too small for Dad's liking. And like a spite I wohn get bigger.'

'Why d'you steal?'

Neil shuddered faintly. Then he suddenly smiled, but stayed silent.

'Why did you smile? What was the feeling that made you smile?'

'It shocked me, mam — that — that I suddenly know why — why I swipe things.'

'Why then, d'you swipe things?'

Neil sighed. 'I — I wahn to have more, mam.'

'More of what?'

'Jus' more. More of anything to make me bigger.'

'You *will* get bigger! Your father here was once your size. And one day you'll be as big as he is.'

Neil shook his head. 'No, mam.'

'What d'you mean "no"?'

'My dad was never my size and I'll never be his size.' Everybody laughed.

'In your own way then, you'll get bigger,' Mother Eesha said. Neil smiled again. She explained to Neil how she believed every name had a secret personal Name-Story. And would he like to hear his personal Name-Story?

'Yes, mam,' he said quietly.

She told him she had to wait till it came into her head, in the form of a poem. She closed her eyes. And Mother Eesha was obviously thinking hard. Her lips began to move. She said:

Here's a Name-Story to be heard

about this special special one-word —
about a finder of what will fit
who takes a problem and works at it
who is warm or cool or hard like steel
who carries the sound-sign that says NEIL!

Neil was very thrilled. He grinned as if he couldn't stop. He looked as if he would ask Mother Eesha to say his Name-Story again. But Mother Eesha said, 'I cahn say it again. I don't remember it. But if you *think*, you'll remember it. And then you can write it down if you like.'

Straightaway Mother Eesha told Neil about the other secret and mysterious thing she found she could do for children. It was being able to read something that was written in their grown-up diary. Neil wanted a Grown-up Diary Reading. So again Mother Eesha closed her eyes. That look of deep, deep thinking came over her face. And Mother Eesha said:

MY BIGGEST MONEY-MAKING DAY

Hurray! Today I did it. Today I broke my best money-making record. For the first time in one day I made one hundred thousand pounds, buying and selling houses. Big and beautiful old houses!

People don't seem to know anybody can make lots of money. People don't know there are only a few rules to follow. But then, it was as I went along that I myself found my own six simple rules. And what are those rules for my money-making?
1: You must really want to sell something to make a profit.

2: You must like a line of business that supplies a demand.

3: Deep down, know you are going to succeed, come what may.

4: Be totally dedicated to your business.

5: Keep a sharp eye for the opportunity to expand.

6: Get your staff to like and enjoy working for you.

Neil's eyes shone like stars, with an amazing far-away look in them. 'What a wonderful, wonderful secret!' he barely whispered — 'wonderful!' He looked at his parents, wishing they'd never tell this secret to anyone. Yet, he said nothing to anybody — nothing else.

When the family left Mother Eesha's place, the parents were well on their way, thinking up ways they could be different to Neil — particularly his dad.

Next, Wendy and her dad sat with Mother Eesha at the low glass-top table.

Wendy's dad said, 'Mother Eesha, Wendy won't eat. You see how flat and thin the poor child is. She's like two sticks walking. My lovely, lovely Wendy! She forces herself to eat. And jus', jus' brings it all up. I take her to see a specialist. But, so far, no change. None.'

'How does she get on at school?'

'Perfect,' her father said. 'Wendy's usually tops in her Year.'

'And in her spare time? What she does?'

'Reads, reads and reads adult books. Plays the piano.

Or spends her time petting or over-caring for the cat. Slightest excuse and the poor animal has to put up with having a paw bandaged. Or taking medicine. For my part, she doesn't talk enough. Though she's good at it. And sometimes she amazes me how knowledgeable she is. Yet with her music, her scholarly ways, her helpfulness, Wendy's great company. But, I have to say, I do wish there was more of the child about her.'

'Wendy?' Mother Eesha said.

Wendy fluttered her eyelids and opened her eyes wide. 'Yes.'

'Why you wohn eat?'

Wendy scratched her head lightly, delicately. 'I – I – I dohn know.'

'No idea?'

'No.'

'What does the empty hungry feeling say?'

'It knows it's not a friend.'

'Then how d'you put up with it?'

'I – I dohn know.'

'You're very intelligent. You're a thinker. What reason you see for keeping a condition that's like an unwelcome friend?'

'Perhaps – somewhere – somewhere I feel there's too, too much cruelty in the world, to grow up to,'

'So?'

'So – I'd rather not grow up.'

'Have you always understood it like that?'

'No.'

'When did you understand it like that?'

'Jus' now.'

'So your father didn't know?'

Two teardrops slowly swelled up and fell from Wendy's eyes. 'No. I didn't know. He couldn't know.'

Mother Eesha looked at Wendy with a deep sympathy. She waited, allowing Wendy to dry her eyes. 'Okay now, Wendy?'

'Yes, mam.'

'Tell me, don't you like reading stories for children?'

'Only when I mus' for school.'

'What's it about grown-up books that makes you prefer to read them?'

'I started when I was nine years old and never stopped.'

'Why you dohn jus' read children's books?'

'It's grown-up books draw me to them, mam.'

'What in them draws you to them, Wendy?'

'Westindies history. And people stories. All bad and cruel and awful and terrible and sad. And, mam, they kind of haunt and compel me to find and read more and more of them.'

'And the feelings you described are the only feelings you find in the grown-up stories?'

'Yes, mam. Feelings — cruel and bad. Hurtful — and horrible. Like a sucking-down swampland that holds you in darkness to drown you.'

'How, d'you think, a lot of grown-ups manage to live till they are old?'

Wendy was surprised. She glanced at Mother Eesha and gave a little smile. 'I dohn know, mam. I really dohn know how they happen to manage that.' Wendy laughed.

'It's your father who brings you. Why didn' your mother come too?'

'Mamma and Dad divorced. Mamma lives in Canada.'

'You see her sometimes?'

'Yes, mam. But I dohn wahn to much.'

'So you and Dad and the cat and the piano live alone?'

'We have a housekeeper with us — Miss Pimm. Miss Pimm is good to me. She teaches me to make a cake and iron properly.'

'So you know now why you wohn eat?'

'I — I know, I dohn wahn to die because of Dad.'

'So what you going to do?'

'I think — I think I'll know when I talk to Dad.'

'And — you think — he'll understand?'

Wendy nodded. 'Yes. Yes. I think so now.'

Mother Eesha explained to Wendy how she believed every name had a secret personal Name-Story. Wendy was keen to hear hers.

Mother Eesha closed her eyes. Wendy's Name-Story came like this:

> Here's a Name-Story to be heard
> about this special special one-word —
> called in bad temper and in soft whispers,
> called for a joke and to work,
> called for a dance and to silence,
> called to sobbing and to prizegiving —

that 'Wendy!' 'Wendy!'
a real friend of the speechless many.

Wendy smiled a smile of someone who never expected to be surprised pleasantly. Her dad smiled too. He'd not seen such a happy look on Wendy's face for a long time.

Wendy wanted a Grown-up Diary Reading as well. When Mother Eesha closed her eyes, this was what she said:

THE SICK DONKEY I TREATED PRACTICALLY TALKED TO ME

Today I felt both sad and happy at the same time. Nothing makes a vet feel better more than seeing a sick animal recover. Janey, the donkey, was taken home today. Half-dead when she came, today she looked, oh, so much better. So much more rounded up with a strong steady walk! But she didn't want to go.

Time to go and Janey looked at me with plead-ing eyes. Her look at me, said, 'Oh please, please, keep me here in your backyard with its green grass and little houses. Don't let my owner take me away with him again. Don't let him take me. I'll die this time! Away from here, each day brings a heavy load on my back, in hot sun, seeming only up and up stony hilly ground, on and on. I'll die under my burden of heavy load. I'll die this time!'

Sorry, Janey. A vet's job is to help animals, treat them and get them well for themselves and their owners. But when an owner is poor and keeps an animal overworked, even when tired and ill, it is very, very sad.

Tonight, Janey, I'll support your rebellion. When I play the piano for myself, tonight, I'll play my favourite rebel song for you, on your behalf.

Wendy cried. Her dad comforted her. She couldn't stop crying.

When they got into their car, he said, 'Wendy, it's a long time since I've seen you cry. It's good to cry. It's good to cry like this. We understand this so much better now. Don't you feel so?'

'Yes, Dad. Yes . . .'

Day after day the Future-telling Lady went on helping children and their parents. Her particular gifts helped them to see and understand their problems for themselves.

Mr Mongoose and Mrs Hen

AUTHOR'S NOTE

When I was a child in my Jamaican village, I heard the story of 'Mr Mongoose and Mrs Hen' told with the characters of Sis Goose (as Mrs Hen) and Brer Fox (as Mr Mongoose). Later, I discovered in London that the story was, in fact, an American folktale; it appears to have been first collected and published under the title 'Old Sis Goose' (from Brazos Bottom Philosophy, *A. W. Eddins, 1923). My story, with its setting in Jamaica, develops the allegory of the original.*

Mrs Hen was happy, six fluffy and beautiful chickens had come under her, and all about between her feathers, after three weeks of sitting on her nest. Out in the big yard for the first time, a proud mother, her six chicks peep-peeped around her. Mrs Hen clucked all the time, protectively, caringly, happily, every chick close to her. But, O, unhappiness waited for her. Though the last idea Mrs Hen would ever have was that somebody was somewhere all ready to turn her happiness into misery.

That Mr Mongoose peeped through the fence and saw Mrs Hen with her new chickens. And Mr Mongoose weighed everything up. Mr Mongoose looked

to see who was about. Mr Mongoose hid himself and
waited for everything to be exactly the right moment.

There in her yard, Mrs Hen was totally taken up
with mothering her fluffy first-day chicks. Mrs Hen
searched and clucked, calling her chicks to hurry and
see who'd be the first to take any bits of food she'd
found.

Mr Mongoose, careful not to be seen, strolled up
into the yard as if he knew nothing would stop him.
Then, with one straight reckless dash, Mr Mongoose
charged right into the middle of Mrs Hen and chickens.
Everything feathers and panic and terror, mother and
chicks hollered and scattered, screaming. Nippily,
cockily, as Mr Mongoose came, he left again. Vanished!
Was gone! Shattered and stunned as she was, Mrs Hen
turned here, turned there, calling her chicks together.
In her terror, Mrs Hen moved quickly to the other side
of her yard, with frightened chicks trying to keep up
close beside her.

Mrs Hen comforted her chicks. She sat down. She
got the chicks to nestle safely all around in her tummy
feathers. But, clucking, clucking, calling, Mrs Hen knew
one chick was missing. She knew – oh she knew – Mr
Mongoose had gone off with one of her babies. Yet
she couldn't stop calling. And that sound – that sound
of Mrs Hen's calling – was the sad sound of a distressed
mother.

Unexpectedly a voice spoke to Mrs Hen. 'Awful,
isn't it? I know. I know how terrible it is.'

'You do?' Mrs Hen said, looking up and seeing Mrs
Ground-Dove sitting on a low branch. 'I'm shattered,'

Mrs Hen went on. 'Shattered. Thank you for saying something. Thank you so much.'

'I saw it all,' Mrs Ground-Dove said.

'You saw it happen?'

'I saw it happen.'

'What then can I do? Oh, what can I do?'

'Nothing,' Mrs Ground-Dove said.

Alarmed, Mrs Hen said, 'Nothing? Nothing I can do?'

'Nothing,' Mrs Ground-Dove said. 'I lost my whole family to that beast Mr Mongoose.'

'Your whole family?' Mrs Hen gasped.

'My whole, whole, family,' Mrs Ground-Dove said, 'And I tell you, I myself have to be careful. Have to be very careful. He's taken friends of mine. Taken them! And tried after me, too. Tried to turn me into feathers. Yes, he's tried.'

'This is dreadful,' Mrs Hen said. 'Dreadful. Do – do – if you hear, hear about anything – anything – that can be done, let me know. Please.'

'I will. I will,' Mrs Ground-Dove said and flew away.

Next morning Mrs Hen made sure she didn't take her babies to the same side of the fence as yesterday. But soon, so taken up in finding little extras for her chicks to eat, Mrs Hen found herself and family charged into again. Leaping into the air, Mrs Hen came down with wings flapping, ready for a fight, but Mr Mongoose was gone. Crying chickens were scattered everywhere. In her own state of terror, Mrs Hen collected her babies together behind her and again hurried away from the spot of attack.

Her chickens were under her, comforted between her feathers. But Mrs Hen clucked anxiously, knowing she'd lost another chick. Yet, worse was to happen.

In all, for six days, every day, Mr Mongoose strolled into the yard and carried off and ate one of Mrs Hen's chickens.

On that awful final morning when her last baby had been carried off, Mrs Hen was thrown into a kind of madness. Her hurt was more than a terrible sadness, for herself and for the pain of her lost chicks. Her loneliness was strange and peculiar. Without her chickens, the last one gone, it was as if she couldn't see, feel or hear anything and didn't know how to be her-self. She found herself going about the yard, clucking, calling. Then she found herself searching for her old nest. Mrs Hen came to it and stood over it, looking in. She stepped into the old nest and sat down. Empty of eggs, empty of chicks, the nest was peculiar. It offered no peace, no comfort. All silly and miserable, Mrs Hen gave up the sitting and walked about the yard, clucking, calling, wishing for a miracle that'd make her chickens appear.

A voice came from nowhere. 'So, you're like me now,' it said.

Mrs Hen looked up and saw Mrs Ground-Dove on a low tree branch. 'Yes,' she replied. 'I'm like you now. My whole family! My whole family! I've lost my whole, whole, family ... What can I do? What can I do?'

'You could take that beast Mr Mongoose to

court,' Mrs Ground-Dove said. 'You could take him to court.'

Mrs Hen looked away in great, great surprise and wonder. She'd never thought of taking Mr Mongoose to court. 'Yes,' she whispered. 'Yes! That *is* something I can do. That really *is* something.'

'It is, isn't it?' Mrs Ground-Dove said. 'I'll watch for the outcome. Good luck.'

Mrs Hen took Mr Mongoose to court.

Mr Mongoose was escorted by a policeman into court. Mrs Hen's charges against him were to do with attack, robbery and murder of her six baby chicks.

Mrs Hen sat waiting for the trial to begin. She was all excited inside. She wanted to make sure she told what happened clearly and properly. She was getting everything orderly and clear in her head, when something struck her. Mrs Hen noticed that every policeman in court was a Mongoose. The clerk of the courts was a Mr Mongoose. The prosecutor was a Mr Mongoose. And the judge – the judge who'd just come in and sat down – was an older and big-bellied Mr Mongoose. Every official who ran the court was a Mr Mongoose! Mrs Hen was shocked, horrified, panic-stricken. She'd never felt more ganged-up against, more exposed, more tricked! Mrs Hen's shock and worry turned into a tight pain across her tummy. Mrs Hen wanted to talk to somebody official. She wanted to talk to somebody!

Mrs Hen pulled herself together, telling herself not to be silly. This was a court of law. It didn't matter who the officials were. It didn't matter one bit who the officials were.

Then, as if everything happened far, far away, Mrs Hen heard the officials of the court using her name a lot. The court was actually in session. Her case had started.

At last it was Mrs Hen's turn to tell her case against Mr Mongoose. She told the court how Mr Mongoose attacked her and her family and robbed her of all her baby chicks. Every day for six days Mr Mongoose came and took away one of her baby chickens. He took all of the six she had. That same Mr Mongoose standing there in court robbed her badly, brutally, and murdered her babies. And not one was left with her. Not one. And she was heartbroken and sad. She was asking the court to let Mr Mongoose repay her for the loss of her family, for their suffering, and for her suffering. And she was asking the court to punish Mr Mongoose. And to stop him from making any such attack on her or on anyone else ever, ever, again.

The court listened to Mrs Hen patiently. The court listened to her till she was completely finished.

Then one Mr Mongoose court official in a gown got up and spoke. And O the Mr Mongoose court official in his gown broke up Mrs Hen's story badly. He broke up her story and changed it badly, badly. And from then on every other Mr Mongoose court official talked about only the broken-up and changed story. And the same Mr Mongoose in the gown began to laugh, saying, 'My good lady, Mrs Hen, how can you actually bring a case like this to court against someone without proof? Without any proof whatsoever!'

'I hope you understand your case, Mrs Hen,' the Mr Mongoose judge said. 'You have no evidence. You have no witnesses to prove that what you accuse Mr Mongoose of is true. You have no witnesses. Do you understand that?'

Mrs Hen did not understand. But she didn't answer. She was too, too shocked and bewildered with disbelief at what she saw the judgment would be. And, truly, Mrs Hen lost her case.

Alone again, Mrs Hen started walking home.

Mrs Hen walked slowly across a field. Dazed, hardly able to move, she walked slowly on and on. Sad, sad, Mrs Hen's loneliness made her feel she walked in deepest darkness in a tunnel underground. And she carried the weight of the world. Her body was weighed-down, awkward, heavy. She could hardly walk. Really, it was her sadness that gripped her. Her sadness held her full of tears that would not come. Her head felt all a-spin. And the same thoughts went round and round: 'Cruelty ...! Dishonesty and cruelty ...! I'm lost ... Lost ... Mongooses have all the say. All the authority. It makes all mongooses say, yes! yes! yes! It makes them feel strong being dishonest and cruel. Their strength's their cruelty and self-deceit – all wrapped, well wrapped, in a pretence that looks like shining respectability ... Cruelty crushed me. O – cruelty crushes you ...! And I have no more words ... I'm lost ... Lost ...'

Unexpectedly, under a tree, a Mr Mongoose stood

in front of Mrs Hen. Swiftly, Mrs Hen was surrounded by one, two, three, four Mr Mongooses. Everything about them was menacing. Every move and look on their faces was set with violence, attack, death. As they were closing in, Mrs Hen looked straight at one of the Mr Mongooses. She whispered, 'But, today – you – you were my judge!'

All four Mr Mongooses held Mrs Hen. They gripped her tight and hard. They killed Mrs Hen. And with noisy celebration, the four Mr Mongooses ate Mrs Hen.

Ajeemah and His Son

That wiping out of Atu and Sisi's wedding was always going to be one of the painful happenings.

It was the year 1807. The Slave Trade was on. By way of that trade, with all its distress, Africans were becoming Caribbean people and Americans. But the sale of Africans as slaves was going to end, in just another year or so. A new British law would stop the selling of Africans. It would stop them being sold to be slaves on plantations in America and the Caribbean.

It was only the 'selling' that would end, not slavery itself. Stopping the selling was a beginning, and a very welcome start to the end of slavery altogether. Yet even that beginning stirred up wild rage, resistance and awful reactions.

The new law soon to be enforced made people who benefited from the trade all angry, anxious and bitter. The new law made plantation owners cry out. It made them furious at the idea of an end to their regular supply of a free labour force. It caused panic among the ship-owning slave traders and the local African dealers. All ground their teeth in fury and rage at the coming end of their money-making from selling slaves. And the slave traders became determined to work with new vigour. They became determined to beat that end-of-slave-trade deadline, when no more slaves could be shipped; they would get and supply as many more slaves as they could in the short time left.

Remember here too, that young people and children came into the slave-treatment, all the time. They too had to endure a life of no freedom for their parents and for themselves. All was personal for them. The teenage couple Atu and Sisi came into it. They were going to have to face their wedding plans ruined — gone, wiped away as dust.

Truly, European slave buyers would buy. Truly, African traders would obtain the prisoners for sale into slavery. They would find them, even if they had to make their own riots and wars to get prisoners to sell. The slave-trader groups geared and equipped themselves. Their surprise attacks became more unstoppable in the villages. Yet, with all that hidden trouble about, people simply had to go on living their lives.

It was the sunniest of afternoons now. Bird singing filled the day. All unconcerned, Ajeemah and his son Atu walked along their village road in a happy mood. The eighteen-year-old Atu was soon to marry. He and his father were taking a dowry of gold to his expected wife's parents. Going on, not talking, Ajeemah and Atu walked past groups of huts surrounded by bare ground with domestic animals and children playing. They passed fields of yam and corn growing robustly. Atu was thinking about getting married. He knew their coming marriage delighted and excited his sixteen-year-old bride-to-be, Sisi, as much as it did him.

'My father Ajeemah,' Atu said, 'isn't it really some-thing that two other fellows — two others — also wanted to be Sisi's husband?'

Ajeemah didn't look at his son, but a faint smile showed he was amused. 'This bride-gift of gold I carry,' he said, 'will make Sisi's parents receive you well, as a worthy son.'

'I thank you, my father Ajeemah. I know it's your good fatherhood and good heart that makes it possible.'

'More than my good heart, it's my thrift. My thrift! You know I'm good at not losing, but keep adding to our wealth.'

'I know, my father, I know. I should have said, may you continue to have all blessings.'

'And you, my son Atu. May you continue to have all blessings.'

'Thank you, my father Ajeemah.'

'Your mother smiles to herself when she thinks of your coming union with smooth-skinned and bright-eyed Sisi! Good singer, good dancer, that Sunday-born Sisi! Delights everybody!'

'Plays instruments, too.'

'Oh, yes, yes.'

His eyes shining, Atu said, 'She's the best. She pleases everyone. She pleases me.'

'Pleases everyone,' the father agreed. 'Pleases you.'

'And two other fellows shan't get her.'

The father smiled, repeating, 'And two other fellows shan't get her.'

'I'm happy your first wife my mother is happy.'

'Your mother is happy because you'll begin to live

your manhood. And she waits for new children you and Sisi will have.'

'And I'm nervous.'

'Nervous?'

'Yes. I'm nervous of all the preparations and ceremonies to get through.'

'That's usual. Marriage makes even a warrior nervous. Especially first marriage.'

'I'll try to enjoy being nervous.'

'Wisdom, wisdom, from young head!'

'Thank you, my father.'

'Atu, when we get to Ahta the twin – Sisi's father's house – watch his face. Watch for the look on his face. First when he thinks I'm empty-handed. Then next when he sees me lift the two pieces of bride-gift gold from the inside of each sandal I wear.'

Everybody knew Ajeemah worked in leather and all kinds of skins. In the village he was called 'Skinman'. He preserved animal, alligator and snake skins and made sandals, bags, belts, bracelets, knife sheaths, ornaments, talismans and pouches for magic charms and spells. But Ajeemah was also known for his practical jokes. He'd chuckled to himself, thinking up the way he'd present Atu's dowry in a most individual and unusual way. He'd created himself the special pair of leather-stringed, lace-up sandals with thick soles. Each sandal had a space under the insole to fit and hide the bride-gift gold in, while he walked to Sisi's house. Ajeemah's big joke was that he'd arrive as if empty-handed. Then, while talking, he'd simply take off each sandal, lift up the insole and produce his gift by surprise.

But Atu wasn't at all sold on the idea.

'My father Ajeemah,' Atu said, 'suppose Sisi's father Ahta the twin is displeased, and things go wrong?'

'True, my son Atu. If Ahta the twin is displeased that would be a disaster. But Ahta'll not be displeased at all! With the sight of gold for him, Ahta's grin will split his face in two.'

Atu laughed with his father. Won over, Atu now enjoyed his father's scheme along with him. Laughing together, they came round the corner of the footpath, between high bushy banks on each side of the track. And ambushed, with total surprise, Ajeemah and Atu were knocked to the ground, overpowered, by a gang of six Africans with two guns, two dogs, and knives and sticks. With lightning speed, three of their fellow Africans tied Ajeemah's arms behind his back, tightly bandaged his jaws — so he couldn't cry out — and shackled his legs with a chain. The other three tied and shackled Atu in the same way. Then, to allow them to see and breathe but not be identifiable, the kidnappers put a bag — a dirty, sickly stink-hood — right down over the captives' heads and faces.

The kidnappers stood now and stared at the older man. Ajeemah had on more than just a loincloth and his special sandals. Ajeemah wore his magic-spell amulet like a black leather armband. And he wore a flamboyant jacket made of the whole skin of an animal. The front of the jacket was held together with a stringed snake-skin lace-up; the sides were netted with round and square holes; the back was lengthened with tails of monkeys and lions all round. The leader and his second-in-command both carried the guns. They also spoke the other kidnappers' language and Ajeemah's. The second-in-command said to Ajeemah, 'All dressed up, eh?'

The bushy-bearded leader had thick-set shoulders and short, bulky thighs and arms. He walked with a waddle. Admiring Ajeemah he took a few steps round him and said, 'Yeah. Looking like a proper local prince.'

'Ain't he just,' the second-in-command said, undoing Ajeemah's jacket to take it off him. 'This'll do me very nicely!'

'Wait!' the bearded leader warned him. 'Wait! You better watch it!' And he and the others pointed to the magic-spell amulet Ajeemah wore like an armband. 'Take one thing from them,' the gang leader kept on, 'and you begin to rot. Every day you wake up a bit more rotten and deformed. A hand falls off. Then another. A leg dries up. An eye closes. Never again to mend. And you're driven raging mad. Haunted, till you just go dumb. Not a word ever again to come.'

Horror, awe and dread blanketed the kidnappers' faces. The hand of the second-in-command fell from Ajeemah's jacket as if the words he heard paralysed it. He commanded, 'Get moving!'

Eaten up with rage, with everything in them saying, 'strike back!' Ajeemah and Atu stood their ground. Blows with a stick rained down on their backs with cutting pain.

'Hold your stick,' the waddling leader said. 'These two are real specials. There's a top price to be demanded for them. We mustn't damage these strong, good-looking bodies.' He signalled the dogs. And growling with a menace that killed, the dogs leapt up and gripped the captives as if ready to butcher them, till called off. Ajeemah and Atu obeyed, and found themselves walking. And with their hands tied, their legs chained, from that moment Ajeemah and Atu would experience treatment they never believed possible. The kidnappers took Ajeemah and Atu through a wood down to the river. A canoe waited at the bank of the river, guarded by another two men with a gun. Four other men and two women were there, shackled and tied together, lying down in the very large canoe.

Ajeemah and Atu had their hoods removed. Made to get into the canoe too and lie down, they had their legs tied to the others. The canoe moved off. Ajeemah remembered his gold in a terrible fright, while his ankles were handled. At first he thought he might have lost the gold, then that his guard might have wanted to steal the sandals.

Ah! he said to himself. I still have it! I have Atu's bride-gift gold. I still have on my sandals! That's a good sign. This bride-gift is for my son's bride and goodwill for their children. For nobody else. Nobody else must ever get this gold. I must guard it. Always! First chance, they'll break free! First chance!

The canoe sailed and stopped several times. Sometimes it waited a long time till other captives were brought. Eventually the canoe was full.

Night came down. Like all the others with them, Ajeemah and Atu were parched with thirst, were empty with hunger, were stifled with heat. They were weak.

But they were taken from the canoe, hands tied and ankles chained. They were made to walk a painful, killing distance in dim lantern light to their overnight stay in hard, bare, prison-like barracks, where they were given tiny bits of food and very little to drink.

Next day they travelled early, and arrived at the coast by dusk. They found themselves taken into a hot, airless, stinking old fort full of other captives. Well guarded, everybody was in some body pain or plain misery. With many hundreds there together, chained up, sitting or lying on the floor, the place was a horror of groaning, crying, swearing and noisy gloom. Everybody was in terror over what was going to happen to them.

Next morning, after eating, Ajeemah and Atu found themselves going through the strange business of being oiled up to look clean and shiny for display for sale. In many ways they were lucky. Their trader had put them with a specially selected lot of youthful and strong-looking men, to attract highest price.

Ajeemah was getting oiled by helpers when the bushy-bearded leader of the kidnappers waddled up, supervising.

'Hello, chiefman!' Ajeemah called. 'Chiefman!'

He looked at Ajeemah. 'What?'

'A word with you.'

His gun hitched up on him, the bulky-limbed, bearded African came close and asked, 'What you want?'

Ajeemah said, 'Where am I going? What's going to happen to me?'

'Don't worry. You won't be eaten.' The kidnapper slave trader said that because of a long-standing belief circulating among captives that white men bought them to eat them.

'Then, tell me, how long will I be away?'

'It's up to your buyer to tell you that.'

'I beg you, do a kind favour for me.'

'What's that?'

'Do, get a message to my women and children for me. Tell them, Ajeemah — Ajeemah and Atu — say we'll be back soon. First chance! First chance we'll be back.'

'Forget it. I don't even know where you come from.'

'Remember where you got me and my son? Remember? Ask! And get a message to Ahta the Twin — father of my son's bride-to-be. Tell Ahta — '

'Forget it, man. Forget it! I don't know where you come from.'

'I'll tell you. Get a message and I return a good deed for you one day. I come from — '

'Listen. Most I can do for you is to get you in with the best captain I can. D'you hear me?' The slave trader began walking away.

Ajeemah was desperate. He shouted, 'You must do something! You must! My four-year-old, my son of birth pangs I shared, my Kufuo, must know I'm coming back. He must know!' The slave trader stood and watched his desperate captive. Ajeemah pleaded more quietly. 'My little fellow must know something. No goodbye linger with us. No last tender feeling exchanged — to sustain us! Say you'll get a message — to my family. Please!'

The kidnapper despised Ajeemah for talking like that. He looked at Ajeemah as if he'd just disgraced himself shockingly. 'You've looked like a prince,' he said, 'and behaved like a warrior, till now.' He waddled away and got on with the supervising of his slaves being made ready for sale. And standing in groups, black faces, chests, arms and legs well oiled and shining, the people were put on show for the white captains of the waiting ships to come and choose their purchase.

Ajeemah and Atu had never seen a white man. They held in their tension and terror and watched the strange creatures. Ajeemah wondered if his flesh would end up in the flesh of one of the white men in captain's hat and high boots.

In a stream of captured people, Ajeemah and Atu were taken on board ship that same day. Other slave passengers were already there. By the end of the day the ship was full of sad, frightened, griefstricken and wildly angry people chained up together. Over three hundred of them, they lay side by side on fittings like layers of shelves.

When the ship pulled away, noisy weeping and sobbing broke out. Screams of terror rose up and ripped through the decks and echoed back to land. And as the coast of Africa disappeared, a long drawn-out groan of grief rose up together steadily from the people one after another, till all died away into silence.

Every African on board belonged to the Captain. He had paid for them all. And they were his goods to resell at stupendous profit, way, way above purchase price. To keep costs down, and sail with as many slave people as possible, the Captain's way would prove to be unprovoked punishment and frightening misery for his cargo passengers. But, for now, all were simply in a state of shock, felt as extreme bewilderment.

All a mixed-up lot — chained to the deck to heavy iron rings — the people were mostly strangers and enemy-tribe individuals at one another's side. Ajeemah and Atu were not together and didn't know where each other was. Atu called out, 'My father Ajeemah? Are you here? My father — '

'Yes, my son Atu. I'm here!'

'My father?'

'Yes, my son.'

'We've both fallen into hell!'

'Into jaws of monsters, my son!'

'Into jaws of monsters, my father! Into jaws of monsters!'

'Always — remember — always, there's a way out. There is a way!'

Neither father nor son said anything else. Each one began to think of his own terrible situation.

Ajeemah remembered the bride-gift gold. Again he'd forgotten it and was shaken with the dread he might have lost it. He moved his toes about — one foot and then the other. Ah! he said to himself. I still have on my sandals! I have Atu's bride-gift gold! Ajeemah thought how sometimes he'd forgotten the sandals for long stretches of time. But, every time he could, he'd tightened up the strong leather-stringed sandals' laces. 'The bride-gift is safe. It's a good good sign!' thought Ajeemah to himself. A really good omen! I lost my jacket when I was oiled. I looked – and it wasn't there! Somebody took it. Just walked off with it. But – Atu's marriage gold is safe! As long as I'm safe, it's safe!'

'Oh, how guns, dogs and mighty kingdoms smash up a man! Smash up his manhood and cut up his pride! They've scourged me and want to make me a disgrace. Oh, I won't let it. I won't let it. They want to take away my manhood and nationhood and add them to theirs. They want to take away all my days and nights and add them to theirs. I won't let it. I won't let it. Kingdoms and individuals are bandits who attacked me and my son. They've reduced me. But they won't disgrace me any further. The good sign of Atu's bride-gift is with me. And I'm far from dead. Far from dead!' Ajeemah opened his mouth to call out to Atu to tell him the sandals were intact and all right. But he changed his mind. 'I better not,' he told himself. 'I must give away no hints whatsoever. Gold is gold! And it's Atu's marriage gold, for goodwill. Goodwill towards Atu and his children, from me, his father. So I must defend it, till – somehow – the right intention is done. All powers in me well know, I will kill, or be killed, in defence of this gold! It is Atu's marriage gold!'

While Ajeemah was there thinking about Atu's gold, Atu himself was thinking about the girl he planned to marry.' ... Oh, Sunday-born, Sisi! Sisi! What will become of our wedding day? You were to be my first wife. And here I am at sea chained up in pain, on a creaking ship, going where I do not know ... I must take everything about you with me. I must remember every detail of your face. Take you in my head so you're with me. And you keep my company. And your walk, your talk, your gestures, your laughs and giggles, like your songs and dances, all keep you in body with me ...' And Atu remembered how with friends and family people he and Sisi had entertained, danced and enjoyed themselves in the evenings. As they danced and sang, someone would put in a favoured person's name into the song whether the person was present or not. He would put in Sisi's name. And they danced and sang:

> Come here O
> Come let's play and dance osibi
> Come O Sisi
> Come here O come here
> Come let's play and dance osibi
> Come let's meet in moonlight
> Come here O Sisi
>   Sisi – come here ...

Then Sisi would put in his name:

> ... Come O Atu
> Come here O come here
> Come let's play and dance osibi
> Come let's meet in moonlight
> Come here O Atu
>   Atu – come here ...

On and on they would sing, with someone putting in a favoured person's name.

Sisi was comical. Sisi could make everybody laugh. Sisi's elephant-act song came into Atu's head. Sisi became an elephant. On its own, the elephant hears drums playing. The elephant starts to dance to the sound of the drums. Sisi pushes a bulky shoulder, lifts a heavy foot, pushes a shoulder, lifting a heavy foot, nodding, pushing a shoulder, into a dance, all to the rhythm of the drum-sound the elephant hears:

Dugu-dugu dugu-dugu-dom
Dugu-dugu dugu-dugu-dom
Dugu-dugu-dom, dugu-dugu-dom, dugu-dugu-dom
Dugu-dugu-dugu-dugu-dugu
Dugu-dugu-dugu-dugu-dugu
   Dugu-dugu-dom
     Dugu-dugu …

Unexpectedly, something popped into Atu's head like a spiteful explosion. Suppose one of the other two fellows should marry Sisi! … Suppose! … Suppose she didn't wait till he got back? … Would Sisi do that? Would she? … But then — Sisi wouldn't know whether he was in hell, heaven or under the deep blue sea! She would have no idea where he was! Alarmed and anxious, Atu gave a loud sigh. He couldn't bear it. He couldn't think about it. But his new worry and Sisi's voice in her songs all became parts of the torture of his predicament. Sisi's voice was mixed in with the awful position he was in. Here he was — a chained-up young man in a ship at sea! Atu's eyes became filled with tears. The pain of his chained ankles, his bruising body, all began to tell him he was on a bitter journey. And all the time, bits of Sisi's singing floated in and out of his memory or circled round and round:

Dugu-dugu dugu-dugu-dom
Dugu-dugu dugu-dugu dom ...

Come here O
Come let's play and dance osibi
Come O Atu ...
   Come O Sisi ...
Come here O come here
Come let's play and dance osibi ...
   Come let's meet in moonlight ...

After three weeks at sea, Ajeemah had taken in some terrible new sights. And he had added to himself a whole new range of painful feelings. Having to watch fellow passengers bawled at and struck by white sailors was an offensive abuse that burnt him up with rage every time. And forced into close living with people of enemy tribes was agony that hardly lessened. But having to travel, wretchedly chained in a fixed position, in a stinking hole of a place was hell itself. No wonder at all people vomited regularly and had unexpected bowel movements. No wonder a man and a woman suffocated in the filthy stink of the ship. It was the two meals a day in fresh air on deck that kept everybody alive. It was that tonic relief of fresh sea air that revived everybody. When would he be able to tell his family about all this? When? Ajeemah wondered.

Six weeks of sea travel and Ajeemah and Atu arrived in Jamaica. They got themselves off the ship, limping: all sore, stiff, weak, half dead. To stand on land again and get fresh air was like a cool river-wash in sunlight. The ship had been a foul, stinking, stifling place. And the ship's rolling and rocking, with them chained up in their narrow spaces, had rubbed and bruised and stripped their skin raw. Four people altogether had died and had been thrown in the sea. Both Ajeemah and Atu had lost their magic-spell amulets and didn't even care. But that his stringed lace-up sandals were still there on his sad, heavy feet, was a magic sign that kept a light of hope ever burning in Ajeemah.

Soon, Ajeemah and Atu were displayed separately with others for sale. And quicker than expected, gates were opened and they had the sun-reddened excited faces of the white men planters down upon them like hungry wolves, looking for the fittest and best for their plantations. But, also unexpectedly, the father and son were about to face their most painful and bitter moment.

Atu saw his father leaving, being taken away by a planter while he was held, already bought by another plantation owner. Led along, Ajeemah looked back, calling desperately, 'Atu, my son Atu — freedom! Freedom! Or let us meet in the land of spirits!'

Two hours' ride from Kingston, in the back of the estate's horse-drawn carriage with two other male slaves bought with him, and Ajeemah came to his big and busy New World sugar plantation. Nearly four hundred slaves lived and worked here.

Everybody stepped down from the carriage in the centre of the estate worksyard in a blaze of sunlight. The estate worksyard buildings spread out like a little village. The huge windmill that powered the grinding of the sugar-cane was near the millhouse where the cane was crushed and where its juice was taken and boiled into the wealth-making sugar, and also rum. Then in a close cluster there was the boiling house, curing house, distilling house and trash house. Ajeemah stared at the windmill; he'd never seen a windmill. He then glanced at the many workshop buildings, animal houses and the overseer's and headmen's houses. And, separated some good distance away, he could see the huts — the slaves' quarters. On his other side, not too far away on high ground, Ajeemah saw the dominant white Great House; it stood in grounds of gardens and whitewashed trunks of palm trees and overlooked the estate's sea-like acres of sugar-cane fields with slaves at work.

A look of pride came over the face of the old slave coachman. Smiling and looking proud too, the estate owner said, 'Look! You see how different everything is from Guinea?' And the coachman translated.

Ajeemah came from the country now called Ghana. His face merely stayed serious and unmoved. Here he was, confused, with his body all sore, stiff, tired and painful. His family in Africa didn't know where he was. He and Atu didn't know where each other was. And he'd been taken to this terrifying place. All the well-laid-out orderliness of the place truly gave him a dread. This was exactly the sort of place where tyrant kings imprisoned, ill-treated and executed victims. Ajeemah's hurt made him deeply solemn, deeply sad. His position of no-hope was his anger turned to silent sadness. His position of no-fight-back-allowed was itself the pain of a bitter bitter trap. The journey had made it impossibly difficult for him to work out how to find his return to Africa. He thought of his secret gold; it stirred nothing — stirred no cheerfulness at all in him. But, Ajeemah knew, at the bottom of it all, he'd have to find a way to get back to his family in Africa, or he'd have to take some terrible revenge.

On that same afternoon he arrived, without luggage, without money or friend, Ajeemah was taken to work under Felix, in the saddlery.

Silent and sullen, Ajeemah was taken into the big opened-up work room, cluttered with new hides and all sorts of pieces of leather. He would work on harnesses and saddles: deal with leather-work for the draught mules and horses of estate waggons and carriages. In fact, he would work on the estate's general leather-work needs.

Confusion suddenly swept over Ajeemah. He felt totally lost. A rush of bewilderment had made his mind go blank. For a brief moment Ajeemah didn't know where he was at all. It was like walking into a little dream and out again. He came back to his senses full of leather smells. And he was seeing a woman and three men standing staring at him. The people talked to him and to themselves but he understood none of the language these black people spoke. Then, Felix, the older man who was in charge, spoke to him in something of his own language. Felix spoke loudly in an awful talking-down way. That too only added to Ajeemah's feeling of the strange, the alien and all that separated him off — the new African.

After work Ajeemah found he was housed with

Quaco-Sam and wife and fourteen-year-old daughter in their big hut. Quaco-Sam had been picked out to supervise Ajeemah, a new man: that meant to talk to him, tell him the worst of the facts, watch him, but encourage him to settle down and become a good, hard-working slave. Quaco-Sam understood Ajeemah's language. He had come from Africa as a teenager. From hard everyday sweating in the fields Quaco-Sam had worked his way up to become Head Boilerman and sometimes a field-gang Head Driver. Quaco-Sam drove the workers hard. He snooped and reported on fellow slaves. Quaco-Sam received special gifts of sugar and rum and an occasional pair of cast-off trousers from the estate owner.

On the second night of Ajeemah's arrival, in the darkness of early night, Quaco-Sam and family sat with him outside at the door of their hut. And in two languages — one for Ajeemah and one for his family — the tall, big and deep-voiced Quaco-Sam went on as if he enjoyed reeling off consequences of trouble on the estate. 'All day long,' he said, 'everybody a-talk an' a-talk 'bout freedom! freedom! An' I say, tell me, wha' you know 'bout freedom? Look 'pon them who turn runaways! They live in woods livin' freedom, livin' wild hog life! They always in rags. They always tired, hungry an' a-parch with thirst. An' always, the military at they heel a-keep them runnin'. An' when they get caught — I tell you — they get bring back. An' they get beaten like a chop-up meat. I wahn freedom, yes. But this freedom! freedom! a expensive thing! I still a poor poor man ...'

Quaco-Sam translated what he and his wife said, into African language for Ajeemah. His wife Phibba explained that if you behaved well you weren't flogged. 'Work good,' she said, 'you get no beat'n'. Behave good, you get no beat'n'.' And Phibba went on telling Ajeemah that when an older woman was a gang driver she was in charge of the estate's five-to-ten year old boys and girls. She would drive them to tend, feed and water estate pigs, goats, poultry and pigeons. She would make them clean out the stable, tidy up the corn-house, food-store, sweep up animal droppings, and do general light work anywhere necessary. And she would drive them to tend estate gardens. That woman driver only used a light whip. She herself was driver of a second field-gang. Her gang had the big girls and boys and old men and women, and did most of the hoeing and weeding.

Sometimes she really had to lash somebody hard, Phibba said. 'Work mus' get done! An' in time! If the work not done, me – me – get the beat'n'! ... Me glad glad,' Phibba went on, 'me daughter here not a fiel' han'. That she work as kitchen han' at Great House. Much, much better!'

'Go watch the "Great Gang" at work in a field,' Quaco-Sam said. 'The bigges', stronges' man an' woman through sunrise to sundown, you a-watch the sweatin' mule gang at work. You watch them clear land, dig holes and plant seed cane, cut the ripe cane in crop-time an' work millhouse – night an' day in crop-time – you a-watch work without pay.'

'Everybody 'pon estate here mus' work hard,' Phibba

pointed out with emphasis. 'Everybody *mus'* work hard!'

'True. Everybody. Everybody ... An' understan', Ajeemah, this is a life whey you have no money; you go nowhere; you have nothin'; but you get used to it, a-search fo' you extra little piece a fish-head. You get your portion of rough cloth fo' clothes; you get you once-a-week piece of meat or saltfish; you get you plot a land to grow you own food; you have nothin'; but you get used to it, a-search fo' you extra little piece a fish-head. Understan' that ...'

In three weeks now, this would be the third time the estate owner himself, Mr Fairworthy, called in at the saddlery to see how the new man Ajeemah was getting on. Dismounting and hitching up his horse, Mr Fairworthy came in and said, 'Felix, how's your new man settling down?'

'Very promisin', Massa. Very promisin'!'

The estate owner turned round to Ajeemah. 'A *good place*, here, Justin. A *good* place!' And Felix translated.

Ajeemah looked the estate owner straight in the eye and nodded with emphasis, 'Ajeemah! Ajeemah!'

'No, no!' Mr Fairworthy said, 'Justin! Justin!' He pointed at him. 'You are Justin. Your name is now Justin!' Felix translated Mr Fairworthy as he talked.

Ajeemah sighed and looked away. On Ajeemah's second day at the estate, Mrs Fairworthy had come to the saddlery with her husband and remarked, 'So, my dear, this is our saddlery African just in?'

'Ah!' he'd said. 'My dear, you've just given me an idea.'

'What, my dear?'

'The name, "Justin". We shall call him Justin.'

Mrs Fairworthy had laughed with amusement. And it had been made known that the name of the new African at the saddlery was Justin. Ajeemah hated the name and rejected it; yet it would stick: the long-settled estate population preferred the name to the African one.

Still looking away now, Ajeemah said, 'Massa,' and Felix took up translating him, 'I am unhappy here. I have a little son and oh, it's such a pain not to have him! Tears come like rain in my heart. My family knows nothing of my whereabouts. And I am the pride of my family. Tears, worry and lament now fill my family's days and nights over my vanishing. My women and children plant and harvest food with me. My women and children help me with my proud work in skins. Now — I without my women and children and they without me — all of us are sad. I gave no consent to be here. I was not a prisoner taken at war. I broke no law. I did nothing wrong to be made your slave. Massa Fairworthy, sir, my request is that, at the end of my request now, you arrange that I begin to return to my people. I need my Kufuo. I need a way back to him!'

Taken aback, the Englishman's pink and sweaty face looked cross, as if confronted by insolence. Then his face relaxed, as if wanting to look compassionate as he said, 'Perhaps, Justin, you don't really quite understand. I actually bought you. Paid for you. You're very important to me. You are both my cash-in-hand and my working cash. I bought you because I expected good business out of you. Meaning profit. Now, if you were to buy yourself back, I'd look back for your purchase price, plus profit I expected to make over your whole life. Do you see that ...? You are in no position to bargain, are you?'

Ajeemah's thoughts went straight to his secret gold under the heavy stone step. With no trunk or a bag or anywhere in his room to keep anything, at first opportunity, Ajeemah had moved the thick, heavy stone-step at the back door, dug a deep hole quickly, carefully hid his gold and replaced the rock. 'I could use the gold!' he thought now. 'Could use it to bargain for my freedom!' Then he remembered — without knowing he had some gold, Quaco-Sam had warned him. A slave couldn't own things. Anything a slave managed to get belonged to the estate. The estate could claim it! Once they knew he had his gold, who'd stop them taking it away? Nobody would. Nothing could stop them ...

In Ajeemah's continued silence Mr Fairworthy went on, 'Who knows, Justin. You may well be able to buy yourself free one day. But certainly not yet ...'

Ajeemah still looked at nobody. Mr Fairworthy wondered what he was plotting. New Africans had a way of trying to run away! He said to Felix, 'Explain to him, I say he'll get used to it here. He'll soon see life here is much, much better than Africa. Tell him too, if he ever tries to run away he'll walk straight into the jaws of terrible, terrible beasts. Runaways live the most wretched life. Always on the run in the hills and valleys of the great woods. Our military men are always hounding them. Needless to say, most often they're caught, brought back and have themselves peppered with flogging, in front of the whole estate ... Tell him, in time, before too long, he'll come to settle down and be well contented and happy.'

The new African spoke unexpectedly. 'Well, Massa, help me to be happy.'

'I want to.'

'Well, Massa, help me find my son Atu.'

'Your son?'

'Yes. Atu. He journeyed with me, over the wide sea and the many moons. And I've lost him. You did not buy him with me.'

'Felix, tell him, it's better — much, much better — to think of having other sons here — right here — in this estate.' His words translated, he turned to go but stopped to add, 'Felix, keep a strict eye on this new fellow. Watch him. But help him to settle.'

'Yes, Massa,' Felix said. 'Yes, sir.'

Ajeemah felt trapped. What a world he'd come to! This world kept him in a trap, so it can take everything! Everything ...!

Same day, at lunchtime, twenty miles away, unknown to Ajeemah, his son Atu also made a request like he had. With his field-gang, eating his brought cooked lunch under a tree, he won the attention of his estate owner who'd ridden by and stopped to listen to him. Atu went forward. The estate owner, Mr Nelson, called someone to translate for him.

Atu said, 'Massa, I was to be married, today! Sisi should have been my first wife and I her husband. And

I am here, with pain in my heart for Sisi, my flashing-eyed singer and dancer. Massa, fix it in reverse that I journey back to Sisi. Once she sees me she'll forgive me — forgive my silly absence without goodbye. Let me go back to Sisi, Massa!'

The estate owner looked surprised. He was a little moved and softened. 'Native boy in love,' he said, 'you must know this: there's no going back for you! But, you *will* be all right. Plenty of girls on the estate here! Find yourself another. Pick one. Find one here!'

'Well, Massa — ' Atu hesitated. He went on, 'Help me find my father.'

'Your father?'

'My father Ajeemah. Over the big sea and many moons, we journeyed here together. You did not buy him with me. And I lost him. I lost him, Massa. Will you help me find him?'

'I cannot. You will not find him. Impossible! Remember this: you have a new life. A much better life than Africa. Settle down to your new life. You'll see you like it.' He looked up and waved his hand. 'All these well-behaved people with you here — with happy smiling faces — all were once new like you. All were once new! Now — go back to lunch.' And the estate owner rode away, to his lunch.

Atu was shattered. He stood. What a condemned life I've come into! What an imprisonment called 'happy'! He was sweating, but felt icy, as if his guts had vanished and left him empty.

In bed that night, Atu's head was all full of remembering Sisi. But some other harsh, acrid feelings stuck stubbornly round his memory. Today, at work in the field, he'd been lashed — second time now — for not keeping up with his gang. It was the month of June. All the estate had gone mad with seed-cane planting. And that streaked mark of the cowhide lash across his back was a bitter offensive pain.

'I won't stand it,' Atu said to himself. 'I will not put up with these hurts they call "estate life"! One day — one day — I shall be full and wild and free, reeking revenge!' But those feelings cleared. Sisi came back into his thinking: this was a wonderful relief. So, pleased, Atu grinned.

In his own hard log bed at night, Ajeemah too would fall asleep thinking about the family and friends he'd been wrenched away from in Africa. But that night he faced a terror that seized him from time to time.

Lying on his back, palms of his hands under the back of his head, his eyes facing the ceiling while his dim lamp burned low, Ajeemah was seeing that though he lived, he didn't belong to himself, and didn't belong to the people he loved, and he'd done no wrong to anybody. The truth of his position as a slave gripped him with a chilling horror. It made him feel swallowed by a nasty horrific monster. He was now inside its belly, becoming the flesh of the monster, little by little. What of his future? What of his family? What of this pain and torture, this captivity, giving his life to Mr Fairworthy?

Ajeemah knew he would never save pennies — years and years from the sale of his garden vegetables — to buy his freedom. That freedom was already his very own. He'd decided he would never try to buy his freedom back, as a few people actually did. How then would he get out of his enslavement? How?

In a contrary way, Ajeemah was not at all bitter about his work itself. He'd given himself to his leather work. He loved the joy of handling, shaping and using 'skin'. And his work in leather had improved to a quality he would never have imagined. Also, he quietly enjoyed picking up and learning his plantation English from Felix and others. But his sense of abuse churned him up whenever he was made to go and work in the Boiling House or the waggon-making workshop. Then, always, he knew, he must swallow the extra offence. He must cover up the hammering of his wounds. And he knew that to everybody, he appeared to be settling. For him, everything he did in all this New World business attacked him as a person. Attacked him as a way of life! And he was expected to swallow it! But, as far as he was concerned, all was only temporary. Only temporary! He merely needed more time, to learn and to plan. He needed time to find good, reliable, committed, connections.

The busy round of seasons kept on. It kept on whether it was the making and looking after estate equipment, planting, weeding or reaping sugar-cane and boiling sugar. One demanding time followed another. With all this life of hustle and urgency going on, relaxing time between work and bedtime was short. But Ajeemah turned this little time into his sweet relief of the day. In this soft early darkness of night, alone, sitting on his log stool, his back against his wattled hut, Ajeemah kept in touch, remembering his family and home in Africa.

Sometimes, all the evening, Ajeemah would mourn the loss of his eight children and their two mothers. He would endure the pain of separation from his children, not able to see them, be with them, or hear anything about them, and they too not know anything about him. He would think of the children in order of their ages. He would make a sad groaning sound for everyone, beginning with the first child, a daughter, then Atu, right down to his youngest, Efia, his daughter two years old. Then he would come back to his four-year-old son, Kufuo, and grieve specially, on and on. Sometimes, he merely remembered time with Kufuo.

Last night, Ajeemah came straight to Kufuo. His feeling and imagination strong, Ajeemah saw Kufuo as if he was actually with him in their home in Africa. Grinning, he talked loudly in his African language. He said, 'Man-child – who had me share your mother's birth pangs – have you another handful of red bird's feathers you collected up to give me, saying it's all in your day's work? Eh, little lion? You don't have another handful? Well – the first handful is there. In the calabash. Beside the pieces of snake skin!' He imagined picking up Kufuo and tickling him and enjoying his child chuckles. He whispered to himself, 'Oh, I remember the smell of your breath! I remember your little hand in my big hand!'

Tonight, Ajeemah remembered laughing at Kufuo. And Kufuo, not liking it, said to him, 'My father, you mustn't laugh at me. You mustn't laugh at me.'

He laughed at Kufuo because he wore coils of wisps around his little arm, to imitate his father's amulet. 'I only laugh,' he said aloud, 'because you amuse me. You amuse me because you're such a little man! Such a little man!' And Kufuo was pleased. And, as he often did, Ajeemah settled down, lost in remembered situations and conversations with his son; remembering spoiling him, teaching him to use a spear; remembering them together trapping birds; setting their trap, then hiding, waiting in the wood … remembering singing together and Kufuo's child-voice out of tune; remembering …

Secretly, all the time, Ajeemah looked for somebody to link up breakaway plans with. Reliable connections had to be built! But getting to spot a rebellious, trustworthy soul-mate proved to be a slow process. Mostly, slave people were crushed people; they lived to survive and not antagonise; they crawled for little favours. Ajeemah knew he had to be careful who he talked rebellion with.

And, so – the estate carried on, showing no mercy. The enormous smoke from its furnaces kept on rising towards both the daylight and the night sky. The estate kept up the loudest and most urgent combined noises on the tropical landscape. The estate workshops contrasted clangings and hammerings, wood sawings, animal voices and songs of slaves working. In the vast lake-like fields of sugar-cane, cowhide whips cracked on the backs of work animals and black people washed in sweat. Wheels of cane-laden waggons churned up their field tracks, up to the worksyard, where the sugar-making furnaces roared. And piled-up barrels of sugar, like the piled-up casks of rum, were rolled out, and taken away to the wharfs. And all this was the tune of big profits. And all this happened with the enormous group of seized people, robbed of their lives, treated like work mules. All this permitted the Master to be a kind of king, who accompanied his great wealth to London regularly.

Ajeemah's secret plans began to speed up. Secretly, he'd been seeing Kaleb, a field slave who'd been flogged out of bed to get up and go to work. Separately, he'd also been seeing Mercury, a free-man businessman, who had property and connections.

In the cover of darkness, Ajeemah, Kaleb and Mercury slowly walked up and down the slave-village road. They talked quietly.

'Estate wrong we bad bad,' Ajeemah said.

'Estate block up a man own life way,' Kaleb said, 'an batter him half dead.'

'An' estate get away with it,' Mercury said.

'Nobody — nobody — to stop estate wronging me,' Kaleb said.

'Estate suck life out every slave man, every slave woman, every slave child,' Ajeemah said.

'Half estate belong to slave people,' Mercury said.

'More than half estate a-for slave people,' Ajeemah said.

'An' them will never get it,' Kaleb said.

'Get it?' Mercury said. 'Get it? Fair deal fo' slave? Fair deal fo' slave? Never. Considering fair deal fo' slave would be miracle! Miracle!'

'So we make own court,' Ajeemah said. 'We make

own court. We put estate on trial.'

'Exactly!' Mercury said. 'How else? How else will fairness happen?'

'We mus' make fairness happen,' Ajeemah said, and his voice became deeper and low. 'We mus' pass sentence on estate. An' make sentence happen.'

'I tell you,' Mercury said. 'Listen.' And he explained. At ten years old — forty years ago — he was tricked away from his parents in Africa and brought to this estate. To this day his parents couldn't have had one single word about him. He certainly had heard nothing from them. And thirty years he spent in slavery. Thirty years! And saving 'one-one' pennies for twenty years, he bought his freedom, ten years ago. More excited, well worked up now, Mercury's hands gestured strongly in the darkness. 'Listen, man! I tell you. Understan'. I have black friends an' white friends, clean friends an' dirty friends, big friends an' little friends, law friends an' bush-rebel friends, country friends an' town friends. An' all — every one — believe in freedom! Every one wahn slaves free! Every one! Understan' me? Understan'?'

Ajeemah and Kaleb gave a long and deep groaning sigh.

Ajeemah said, 'I wohn pay fo' freedom. Never! Already that freedom mine when I born. Mine! My freedom get robbed. I dohn pay fo' it back. Me dohn pay robber.'

'Well,' Mercury said, 'I paid fo' my freedom back. With twenty years of saving pennies from vegetables I sell from my food garden I paid. I paid the Englishman for my freedom he said he owned.'

'I wohn pay,' Ajeemah said. 'Me freedom a-for me! Fo' me own self. I get kidnapped. I get seized. Me life is robbed. Me whole life robbed from me. No. I dohn pay fo' it back. I pay no robber. I fight him. Me fight the robber. Fight him!'

The men walked along in silence for a little while, there on the slave-village road, in the darkness. They turned around and walked back again. How loyal and true was Kaleb? Ajeemah had a little doubt about that. He asked him, 'So Kaleb, you really full-full decide?'

'Me?'

'You really wahn come in on the plan with me? An' have a job to do?'

'Come in on the plan?'

'You really really wahn to?'

'You know right now I in pain. Me back raw like a slice meat. Me skin cut up with beat'n'. Gimme the chance, an' you think I wohn pepper estate people backside too? That I wohn pepper they backside? Gimme poison, gimme the way, I poison the lot tomorrow. Massa first! That damn Massa first!'

'Good,' Ajeemah said. 'But, Kaleb, you'll have a gun, not poison.'

'Man, gunfire a quick-quick poison! You say gun dohn make quick poison cut-up? Me say, gun got best rotten-up fo' that Massa belly.'

Mercury said, 'Listen! I meself dohn wahn know what you wahn the guns fo' at all. You give me order fo' twelve guns, twelve horses an' ten rebel fighters, fine! I will supply all that. All made ready an' left somewhere agreed. Guns all nice an' neat in sugar bags. But, understan', my job's only deliver of order. An', of course, collecting me money from you fo' meself, fo' everybody an' everything. Agree?'

'Agree!' Ajeemah said. And decision was reached. This stage of the plan was settled. Mercury would get in touch with Ajeemah again in ten days' time. He would let him know when, where and how to collect all items he ordered.

Ajeemah walked alone in the darkness back to his hut. And, as if he had a fever he had longed and longed for, Ajeemah's excitement roasted him. Things were moving fast now! He told himself: now I can use my gold! Perhaps this is what my gold was meant for. Half my gold will go to pay Mercury. Go to pay for freeing myself! Freeing myself! Oh, Atu, your bride-gift may yet pay for us to meet again! Oh, Atu my son! Oh Atu! But how? How will it happen? How will the plan work? Oh, Atu, I'm going to make drama and confusion and pain for the cruel, cruel ways that rob us, damage us, and keep us trapped!

Ajeemah began thinking about that part of the plan he'd told nobody about. That was the setting of the whole estate on fire at night. Set everything important ablaze. Get the Mill-house, the Boiler-house, the Curing-house, other worksyard buildings, the Great House, and six biggest cane fields, all roaring together, in a glorious all-round upsurge of flames and smoke.

On a moonlight night, six rebel fighters on horse-back would set the six biggest young cane fields alight. Swift on horseback, the rebels would set each field ablaze at its centre and four sides. He, Ajeemah, and Kaleb would set the worksyard houses on fire at the same time with the cane fields. The other four rebel fighters would hide in wait around the Great House. When the flames of the cane fields and worksyard buildings lit up the sky, and Massa and everybody had left, rushed out and away, to stop fires, Great House itself would be set alight. Then the rebel fighters would guard it till it was burnt down to metal, concrete and ashes.

Ajeemah saw it that he and Kaleb would start, hasten and defend the burning-down of the worksyard. They would shoot all who tried to stop the fires. He would let Kaleb get away and free himself. He would stay and shoot it out with Massa and staff and the militiamen when they arrived. Unexpectedly, Ajeemah saw he would be shot and killed. He roared, 'My son Atu, we promised! Make we meet in the land of the spirits! Make we meet up! In the name of freedom, make we meet up!'

Lying on his back in bed, Ajeemah whispered in his African language to his youngest son, 'Ha-hah, Kufuo man-child, what muscles! So big big! When did your muscles get so big! I'll have to do something about mine. To stop your muscles getting bigger than mine I'll have to rub my muscles with special herbs and oils!' And he imagined hearing his little son's tickled laughter. And he himself chuckled. And he began remembering Kufuo's voice, singing with everybody. And with sad feelings, suddenly, Ajeemah remembered — Kufuo would be older now: five years older.

And he remembered too, five years now, he'd lived in Jamaica!

For three days after seeing Mercury, Ajeemah lived in a wonderful dream world of the strong and the powerful. Seen at work, smelling of leather, tanning it, cutting it, sewing it, admiring it, Ajeemah gave no clues he felt ready to die. On the fourth day something dramatic happened.

The estate owner and a militia officer visited Ajeemah at the saddlery. They took him to the book-keeper's house back veranda. They made Ajeemah sit down while they too sat down on benches around him.

The tall, red-faced officer took a piece of torn brown paper from his red-coat pocket. He read the scrawled message:

MASSA STRANGA WAN COME BRIB JUSTIX

His uniform spotless, his manner calm — all as if he didn't represent the law and punishment — the officer kept friendly eyes on Ajeemah. He spoke slowly. 'This written message was dropped over Great House gate, while it was closed. Do you know who might send this message to Massa? With your name on it?'

Sitting there barefoot, in rough slave clothes, with face, chest and arms shiny with sweat, Ajeemah's black face was a blank. He shook his head. 'No, sir. Me dohn know.'

'Has anybody given you money — any money at all — or a gift, for a favour you have done? Or for

anything you are doing, or selling, or planning to do
for him or them? Anybody tried to bribe you?'

'No, sir. No!'

'Now, Justin, tell me. Who might want to tell something on you?'

'Me dohn know, sir.' Ajeemah made himself sound
very certain.

Mr Fairworthy took over the questioning. And his
hair and fingernails neatly cut, his clothes sweaty but
superior and smart, the estate owner's voice was firm
but smooth. 'Justin, why is your name on this message
to me?'

Ajeemah shook his head. His reply firm. 'Me dohn
know, Massa. Me dohn know who send message.'

'No favours asked of you? Nobody wants you to
give him or sell him leather?'

'No, Massa.'

'Nobody wants you to give or sell anything from
another workshop?'

'No, Massa.'

'Have you been talking to anybody — anybody
different or anybody at all — about any kind of business
or matter or anything?'

'Well — yes, Massa. I did want a cow.'

'A cow? A cow for yourself?'

'Yes, Massa.'

'And what happened?'

'I have talk with Mercury fo' cow.'

'Ah! Mercury?'

'Yes, Massa.'

'And what happened?'

'I did hear Mercury sell cow. So I ask Mercury sell me one cow.'

'You wanted a cow for yourself?'

'Yes, Massa.'

'And what did Mercury say?'

'Him say, cos me a slave, I first get permission from estate.'

'Did you ask anybody for that permission?'

'No, Massa.'

'Why not?'

'Too much bother, Massa.'

'I see. Well, when you talked to Mercury, who else was there?'

'Who else?'

'Yes, who else was there?'

'Nobody else, Massa.'

'Nobody else was there?'

'No, Massa. Nobody else.'

'When did you talk to Mercury?'

'Three or four days past.'

'Justin?'

'Yes, Massa.'

'You must tell me the truth. You understand that?'

'Yes, Massa.'

'This officer here will go and talk to Mercury. He will go and see if what you say is true. Telling lies won't help.'

'No, Massa. Lies no good.'

'If what Mercury says is different from what you say, you'll be in trouble. Bad trouble! For telling lies! You well understand?'

'Yes, Massa. Me know that.'

'You still have a chance to tell me the truth.'

'Is truth I tell, Massa. I tell all truth me know.'

'You are not concealing anything you must and should tell me?'

'Me concealing nothing me must tell you, Massa. Nothing.'

'All right. Go on back to work.'

Ajeemah was shattered. All hope to escape was gone! He walked back to his workshop stunned, as if he'd been dealt a killing blow. He walked around lifeless, feeling like his heart cut down into the pit of his belly. His plan to escape was finished! Wiped out! Once the estate suspected you and all their powers landed on your trail, your plan and you yourself were doomed. Done for!

Right away Ajeemah suspected Kaleb. With all of his crying 'sore back', with sharp talk, Kaleb had impressed him only as a poser. Kaleb was like the general run of settled slave people. All beaten down, gutted and trampled, they didn't have the stomach for a fight. Yet Kaleb couldn't bring himself to expose the real planned gun attack on the estate, as he understood it. He merely spilled something enough to get the deadly hounds out, sniffing, and stopping all plans for attack. What a good thing he and Mercury had thought of a watertight protection, for emergency, just in case. What a good thing they'd built in the cow-buying smokescreen, for both to stick to, if questioned. What a good thing, too, they'd decided to deny Kaleb, as a third person present. Once the militia visited him, Mercury would cancel the order he gave him. He would cancel fighters, guns, horses, everything. Mercury understood everything. He would expect to be watched like he, Ajeemah, would be watched day and night.

Deeply disappointed, Ajeemah didn't know what else to do. Everything was hopeless. He became sadder and lonelier. Day after day and night after night, he went only to the leather workshop and to his log bed. He lost the feeling for his imaginary talks with his little son. It became too hard to feel that he saw Kufuo. And he stopped trying. He was full of rebellion he couldn't make work. He was hurt and sad. He was in agony that people could have so ganged up on him and abused him. So ganged up and spoiled his life that he had and wanted! So ganged up and made him a slave! He missed Africa. More than ever he missed his family; he missed his Africa and its way of life. Being a slave so reduced and spoilt a man! So took away all of your own life! So robbed all of you for another man called 'Master'! So kept you as always an unfinished carcase ready for the lion's hunger! And a new longing stormed into Ajeemah.

He was wishing and wishing his people in Africa could read. He wished so much that at least his people could read and he could write and could send them a letter. Oh, he longed to make contact. But, in that wishing, he knew he would live. He had to live. He had to damage the estate that so damaged him. He had to damage the estate and its owner — properly! Yet Ajeemah sank deeper into a sad, sorrowful feeling that wouldn't leave him. And he began muttering to himself, as soon as he was alone.

In his own language, he mumbled to himself. 'Atu! Atu! My son, Atu! They changed my name. Have they changed your name, too? What day are you now born on, and what new name goes with the day? Oh, Atu, I would avenge us alone. But they are clever. They would make me waste the effort. They would let me waste myself for myself altogether. They would see I get no satisfaction for myself at all. But, if I had you with me, Atu! If only I had you with me. We would avenge ourselves together. We would make this place a roaring fire, on every side. A roaring, roaring fire everywhere! And die in it, fighting! Fighting! Fighting! Oh, Atu! Atu! My son, Atu!'

Ajeemah didn't understand estate security. He didn't know the many ways the estate preserved itself safely. He didn't know that rebellion plotting, by a slave like him, was exactly why estates didn't have new slaves together who were related. Just as slaves of the same tribe were deliberately kept apart. And it worked. Keeping relatives and people of the same tribe apart, when new, prevented a lot of trouble. And so, poor Ajeemah had no idea his son Atu was fairly nearby — only twenty miles away on the Nelson's estate. But, different from his sad and miserable father, Atu was going through his days all bouncy, good-natured, happy. He was full of an expectation, full of that fantastic moment he expected to happen.

He would get away. He'd prepared it. He'd set up his secret plan. Any day now would be his breakaway day. Then, away! Goodbye to the Nelson's estate, forever! Off – and Sisi here I come!

Truly, though, Atu was now a different person from the young man he had been. With the life he lived, and being older, he had changed. He'd found himself standing up to punishments for troubles he caused. He had become more muscular, tougher, and even heartless, cruel and sly. But he knew in every way he felt as he always did for Sisi.

Yet, the testing times he'd gone through really marked him. He'd gone through being cautioned twice, for stirring up trouble among his field workers. On three occasions, he'd received lashes for slacking at work in his gang, and encouraging others to do so too. He'd gone through a terrible flogging, for being ring-leader of a dispute, and for threatening behaviour to his Gang-Driver and to the Headman. Atu had come to be known as troublemaker. Yet, whenever he wanted, he could be the leading worker of his cane-field gang. He could put on his estate-pleasing act, though, usually, to conceal something he'd done.

When Atu's worst troubles accumulated, about three years ago, he had stolen a gun. In his great moment of triumph – in his worship of the gun in his hand – Atu discovered the gun had no cartridges in it. And what a really bitter disappointment that was for Atu! But he kept the gun hidden. His desperation to get cartridges mounted. He searched, watched, waited. Searching the Headman's house to steal cartridges he'd twice come near being caught. In fact, once, though, not caught in the house, his movements had come under critical suspicion. He'd been up to something!

Something! What was it? Only the well-organised and clever liar Atu had become enabled him to talk his way out of that one. Atu *had* to be involved in a secret plan of action. So he still tried, planned again and watched and waited for the opportunity to steal cartridges. His strong obsessive feelings drove him on.

At last Atu was surprised to see that the estate had made him into a man he never thought he'd ever be. Considering it, Atu saw that the estate had done everything to him to make him feel, know and become the worst of himself. And he felt full of wanting to throw everything back into the face of the estate. Atu had actually jumped for joy at the reason that spurred and drove him on to get cartridges for his gun. He whispered, 'I must make them feel something from me. *Feel!* Feel *even* a little mashed up. For the big way they make *me* feel mashed up!'

All excited, Atu had jumped out of bed. In darkness in his hut-room, he'd tossed his arms about and whispered angrily. 'Spoil them! I going spoil them like them spoil me! Spoil them like hell! Damage them like vegetable pig half-eat!' Atu punched the darkness. 'Blast them – that Mr Nelson and Mrs Nelson!' He punched the darkness. 'Blast them – that Busherman the Headman and that damn Gang-Driver! Even that Field-Cook woman who cuss me, call me, "uncivilise new African". Blast them! Every one into piece-piece! Piece-piece! Like vegetable pig bite-up an' half-eat!' Atu had walked about in the darkness, elated with his ideas about his dramatic shoot-up at the Nelson estate. 'O, I going walk plenty middlenight. I going walk plenty middlenight. I mus' get cartridge! A little bagful. O, a little bagful will do!'

And Atu was kept going. Everything in him made him feel he now had a goal for himself. Everything in him made him feel and know he couldn't face the estate any more without that goal. Something he himself worked out and wanted to do. All for himself! He couldn't get out of bed at sunrise to go and sweat in the sun till sundown, for nothing. He couldn't dig seed-cane holes, weed cane fields, reap ripe cane, load waggons, roll barrels of sugar and rum on to waggons. He couldn't lift this, lift that. Couldn't yes, sir! yes, sir! yes, Massa! yes, Massa! and rush here and rush there. He couldn't take the whip lashes, take all the subjection for respect with none coming back to him, without a goal of his own. He couldn't face anything more — couldn't live at all — without knowing he would stage a dramatic shoot-up of all the Nelson estate top people. And, he knew, eventually he would get cartridges and another gun. Occupied like this, for himself — waiting, watching, scheming, planning — Atu managed to go to work. Atu avoided having to be flogged out of bed to go to work. Then — all unexpectedly — something else switched Atu into his present plan. And this same thing made Atu wait three years for it to work. Three long years — till now!

Atu bought a young baby horse cheaply: its mother had died. He bought the long-legged and shaky two weeks' old bay horse at Sunday Market from a man who'd bought himself out of slavery — a free-man. Like other slaves Atu had been allowed his plot of land to

grow food for his keep. Allowed also to come to
Sunday Market to sell vegetables and buy other food,
slaves sometimes made and saved enough money to
buy themselves free. Atu was totally taken up with
this little horse. He even managed to persuade the free-
man to take him and his horse home in his mule cart.

Right away, at the back of his hut, Atu began
laughing and talking to the wobbly little horse like a
long-lost friend. He hugged it. He looked into its eyes
and said, 'Hullo!' He held his mouth up to its ear and
whispered, 'Adohfo! Adohfo!' He looked into its face.
'D'you know meaning of Adohfo?' The big eyes of the
little horse looked blank and sad. 'So,' Atu said, 'you
noh know, eh? I tell you. Adohfo is warrior! Warrior!
You small now. But you will be big warrior. You born
in Jamaica. Not hard fo' you to know Jamaica. I noh
born in Jamaica an' is hard fo' me to know Jamaica. I
born in Africa. An' I know Africa! One day, Adohfo –
warrior! – you take me to find ship, somehow, to take
me back to Africa. We agree? ... Good!' And Atu
hugged Adohfo. 'I mus' stowaway on ship!'

Atu bought, begged and stole milk to feed Adohfo
with a wooden spoon, till it supped the milk from a
pan. He stole corn which he pounded to feed his horse.
Atu got up at 5.30 every morning to have time to cut
grass and get water to leave for his tethered colt. And
the animal became the one real friend and companion
in Atu's life.

Happiest time now for Atu since he left Africa!
Wherever he was, a song-memory of Sisi poured off
the tip of his tongue. Waking up or going to bed,

working in his field-gang or walking through the
village of huts, getting feed for the horse or feeding
him, Atu hummed, whistled or sang:

> Come let's play and dance osibi
> Come O Sisi ...

or:
> *Dugu-dugu-dom, dugu-dugu-dom, dugu-dugu-dom...*

Because of Adohfo, coming back to his hut every
day was a happy event for Atu. Glad to see him
too, the horse gave a gentle low-pitched neigh like a
chuckle. And once untethered, he followed Atu about
the yard and stood beside him, anywhere.

Atu had his colt gelded. And how the horse swelled
out in body and put on height astonished Atu. His
Adohfo actually became a real full-size reddish-brown
grown-up horse! Not able to believe it, Atu would look
at the horse and shake his head. Such a picture of a
fellow! His mane and tail were a joy to Atu to comb.
His body was a pleasure to brush down.

Adohfo allowed Atu to ride him as if he took it as
extended fun. But, being cautious, Atu didn't ride the
horse to Sunday Market; he just didn't want to show
off Adohfo too much. For both practice and pleasure
he rode his horse discreetly. Riding bareback, at night,
or in dusky early morning, he regularly ventured from
his dirt track on to the firmer surface of the main road.

Needless to say, Atu's planned escape was now his
whole dream world. The reckless thumping of his heart
all the time now reminded him his way was clear, his

plan firm. His time on the Nelson's estate was up! That very next Sunday morning, between 3 and 4 a.m., he would disappear on Adohfo's back like wind! For good! O, for good! Never ever to return! And no heading for the nearest port, either, where he might be traced. No heading for anywhere other than the city port. There, he would find a way to hide. He would hide till he found a ship to stowaway on. Whatever should happen – no coming back!

On this his last evening in from his slave work, Atu had to hold on to himself. This dangerous and secret excitement was too much. A pressure inside him made him feel his heart could burst. He had to walk about to slow down and keep a grip on himself.

In the dusky daylight of Saturday evening Atu gave Adohfo a good last feed. He stood stroking Adohfo, talking to him. The estate Overseer and Headman rode up to his hut and came straight round to the back where Atu was feeding his horse.

'Simon,' the Overseer said, as they had renamed Atu, 'we've come to take the horse.'

At first, for Atu, everything was unreal like a dream. His face became a blank. Then, almost slowly, Atu's eyes and whole face became a total alarm. 'My horse?' he said. 'My Adohfo?'

'What you thought was *your horse*,' the Overseer said calmly.

'Sir. Is fo' me, this horse!' Atu stressed with his five years of plantation English. 'Is fo' me, this horse! Me buy him, cheap-cheap. All of whole two years' money go on him, sir. What me save from me food I grow in me garden, sir. Me buy him cheap-cheap. Me buy him from a baby horse half-dead. Me look after him, look after him, till now him big. Big-big, sir!'

The Overseer spoke icily. 'A slave isn't allowed to keep a horse. And, Simon, you should know that.'

Atu shook his head. His helpless arms waved. His whole body shook in desperation. 'Sir. Nobody tell me no keep a horse. Nobody tell me!'

'We don't know you're going to break the rules till you break them.'

'Sir. Big Busherman, sir. This, my horse, my horse, everything, everything, fo' me I have!'

'You never really had it, Simon. That's what I'm telling you.'

'Massa Busher, me own money, sir. Me own money buy the horse, a baby half-dead. Me very own-a own-a money, sir!'

'Simon, you yourself belong to estate. The grass you feed the horse on is estate grass. The time you used to look after the horse belonged to the estate. Just as you are estate property, the horse is estate property.'

'Sir. Me look after my horse every day before work-time an' after work-time. Mostly in dusk an' darkness.'

'That was only estate rest-time that you used. That was time for you to rest for work next day. It wasn't your time.' The Overseer looked at the Headman and nodded.

The two men left the yard. The Headman led Adohfo behind the horse he rode. Atu followed. He stopped. Atu was all disbelief, all pain. He stood watching his horse disappear in the dusk of early night, passing the tropical trees.

Atu felt he had lost all speech. As if an explosion had deafened and dazed him, his head was a fuzzy confusion. He felt he couldn't move. Yet his legs took him walking up and down the dusty village road till he went to bed.

Deep and sullen in his work gang next day, Atu didn't speak to anybody. On the following day, to his absolute astonishment, Atu looked up from his work and saw the Headman sitting on the back of his Adohfo! The Headman had ridden up; he talked to the Gang-Driver. Atu stood stunned like a statue with an instrument in his hand. Atu had never seen his horse saddled and in a bridle with bit and reins. Adohfo was spectacular! Atu thought. Spectacular! And *him* is the rider! Fixed intensely, watching the horse and rider, Atu whispered, 'Adohfo! Oh! Oh, Adohfo!' He looked away in deep thought. And Atu continued working.

Next morning, Adohfo was found in the stable lying awkwardly on his side. The horse was in miserable pain. His two front legs were broken. With much alarm and rush-about, soon, Adohfo was shot, ending its pain.

Mr Nelson roared a field marshal's authority at Atu. 'Simon! What d'you know about the injured horse? Did you commit that savagery? Did you break his legs?'

Atu was calm, fatally calm. 'Yes, Massa. Is me do it. Me do it, Massa.'

'And what makes you think you could get away with it? Eh? What made you think so?'

'I dohn look to get away with it, Massa. Me dohn see it so.'

'You had better not see it so. You are going to be punished! Punished! D'you hear?'

'Yes, Massa. Me know that. Me know that, Massa.'

All the estate slave people were brought together in the worksyard. An audience of well over three hundred! And the people were made to watch, as Atu was flogged and flogged severely.

On the fourth day, since Atu lost his horse, another sad scene followed. Atu's body was found sprawling across the Great House gateway. Mr and Mrs Nelson had driven up in their carriage at 2 a.m. from a function in the town. As usual, the driver stopped and climbed down to open the gate. And there was Atu, dressed as he was after his flogging, in his field clothes.

Mrs Nelson stayed in the carriage. Mr Nelson came out and looked at Atu, most crossly. 'How dare him do a thing like this here! Who told him he could do this here? The disrespect of it. The audacity! ... Pull out the long-knife from his chest! Now, drag him out of the way till daylight.' And he settled in the carriage again, finally saying, 'Made more trouble than he was worth.' But as he remembered standing over Atu being severely flogged, he whispered, 'Poor devil!'

Then, there was a strange happening. And nobody could explain it. At the exact moment Atu's lowered body touched the bottom of his grave, his father Ajeemah had an unusual experience. With a saddle in his hand for repair, Ajeemah gave a dreadfully pained cry — and fell backwards. He held himself stricken, as if suddenly wounded. 'Me son! Me Kufuo! Shark eat him up. Shark nyam him! I see him a-swim. I see him a-swim 'pon big sea. A-come to me. An' shark grab him. Oh, shark grab mi Kufuo! An' shark eat him up.'

Felix was not totally surprised, but concerned. He tried to comfort Ajeemah. 'Never mind,' he said. 'Never mind. Whas really the matter? You in pain? Where it hurt? Where?'

'I dohn know,' Ajeemah sobbed. 'I dohn know. Me see like a vision. I see little Kufuo, a-swim, a-swim, 'pon the ocean, an' shark grab him.'

'How you feel?' Felix asked. 'How you feel?'

'No good. No good. No good at all.'

Felix saw to it that Ajeemah was taken to the estate hospital. News went round the estate that the leatherman African had gone mad. That same evening Bella, a Great House servant, went to see Ajeemah.

'Who say you to come see me?' Ajeemah asked Bella.

'Nobody. I meself wahn come. I get permission. So I come.'

Ajeemah had seen this long-legged Bella about occasionally. She always had a superiority beyond everybody else. He looked at her with doubts. 'Why you come see me?'

'What you mean, why? You's a person. An' not well.'

'You did hear militiaman come question me?'

'Everybody did hear red-coat man come question you.'

'What people say, when them hear so?'

'You's a fairly new African. But not everybody suspicious about you.'

'Suspicious me do something bad?'

'Yeahs.'

'You did suspicious of me?'

'Well — tell the truth. I did pick up the note 'bout you, at Great House gate. An' gave it to Massa.'

'You did pick up the note?'

'Yeahs.'

'You see me name on it an' give it up?'

'Me didn't see you name.'

'Didn't see it?'

'No. Me cahn read, you know.'

'You born Jamaica. Live at Great House. An' cahn read?'

'Yes,' Bella said. 'True.'

'We must get practise quick-quick. Me must know to read an' write.' Ajeemah was thoughtful.

'You?'

'Yes. Me.'

'Good-good ambition. Plenty-plenty of we would like to read an' write.'

'Backra people wohn let it. Wohn let it. Them will say, Nayga wohn work 'pon estate when them can read.'

'Backra people dohn have to have *all* the say *all* the time. Like you, I going learn reading.'

'You born here. An' still wha' happen is wha' you do fo' them. Is crumb from they mouth you get.'

'Justin? Everybody know you is a skill man. An'

plenty-plenty people think you make you life too, too selfish.'

'Me? A man who selfish.'

'Well – I meself – I think you keep youself too much to youself. An', really, you not going back to Africa. You not going back, you know.'

Ajeemah was alarmed. 'Me? No going back?'

'Yes, Justin. You not going back.'

'Me live in Jamaica fo' all me days to come?'

'Yes. One day we all, all, get freedom.'

'Freedom I use to go home. Back to Africa.'

'You won't. No Nayga in Jamaica go back to Africa. Nobody go.'

Bella's words sank into Ajeemah like a command, a revelation, a truth, but also an accusation. Though he knew nobody who went back, her words would find no acceptance in him. He was firm. 'This land – this land – no, no burial place fo' me.'

'Plenty African bury here. Plenty. But fo' you, Justin, before that day come, plenty-plenty can happen fo' you.' He looked at Bella with a gaze that was strong and long. Something between a man and a woman had clicked. And her face, her body, her whole presence sent a warm happiness through him. In a quieter voice, Bella said, 'I bring you a piece a Great House cake. An' some milk with honey.'

Ajeemah and Bella became great friends. Knowing Bella changed Ajeemah drastically.

Bella was ambitious. She longed to get her freedom and get her own home and land. She could not persuade Ajeemah to let both buy their freedom. Ajeemah was absolutely against ever paying anybody for his freedom. But once he felt and began to enjoy a wonderful new sense of partnership with Bella, he too desperately wanted to secure a way to get his own land. Bella was a long-established servant at the Great House. As a slave she enjoyed a special status. She began to use her influence to win ways to get land, when they were able to buy. She encouraged Ajeemah to begin making sandals and shoes to sell. Ajeemah also began to increase his food-growing on his garden plot of land. And this friendship with Bella encouraged him to make his takings at Sunday Market show an increase.

Ajeemah and Bella were married thirteen years after he arrived in Jamaica. He was then forty-nine years old. One year later he and Bella had a baby daughter. The day the girl child arrived on was practically unbelievable. The child was exactly another Sunday-born child, as Atu's lamented Sisi was. Surely, the voice of fate and destiny was clear and eloquent! Surely, a hidden mystery pointed a finger where something special should happen! Naturally, Bella and Ajeemah gave their baby girl the name Sisi. And slow-paced change kept on arriving into Ajeemah's life.

Slave owners didn't want the proposed law to end slavery ever to get passed. But with all their terrible attacks on it, their bitter rages and planned resistances against it, the slavery-abolition law won through and was passed victoriously. But for loss of property, the ex-owners of British West Indies received twenty million pounds from the British Government. And Mr

Fairworthy and Mr Nelson took their handsome share. Yet it seemed the ex-owners would stay angry and bitter forever, never able to acknowledge the people's lives they had dispossessed and lived on. Essentially now, though, freedom — freedom! — had come for Ajeemah, like all the other slaves. And here he was, numbered in with the last generation of people who emptied their work lives into other people's bank accounts. Here he was, in with those who had ended their people's two-hundred-year bondage.

Now an unbelievable first-day was coming. Ajeemah and Bella, with the other estate slave people, waited up all night to welcome their first-day of freedom. They waited and greeted the dawn with singing and joyful prayers of thanksgiving. They cheered and sang till dawn became the broad daylight of 1st August 1838, and open celebrations could begin. Singing sad songs, the ex-slave people collected together, and, slowly together, they moved away from the estate.

Some of the former slaves went and joined the few established free people. Others began putting together their own new villages.

At nineteen years old, in 1840, Sisi was married. In white bridal gown, on the arm of Julius, son of Quaco-Sam and Phibba, she left their church ceremony. They came to her parent's home, a very crowded place. People were still intoxicated with their new-found freedom, setting up homes, and getting land, and learning to be free citizens. Ajeemah had opened a shoe-making and repairs business in their new village. Bella had become a village seamstress. And a wedding reception at their home on this gloriously sunny afternoon was a specially happy occasion.

Ajeemah's suit material had come from England. He dressed like a wealthy estate owner. Beginning his speech, Ajeemah welcomed everybody. He went on and said, 'I'm now sixty-nine years old. I was taken from my motherland, Africa, thirty-three years ago. Plenty things happened since then. Plenty plenty! But first best thing for me, was that special day when I went mad. An' a person I'd only seen going about, came to see me, to nurse me, with cake, an' milk an' honey. What a wonderful day, when in my madness I looked in Bella's eyes, an' I saw love! Such a lonely man I was! I tell you, I never forget my family in Africa. Sometimes, fo' them I shed a quiet tear. But I've made such big treasure chests of new memories. Through Bella! And Sisi. And all good friends here. With Julius now added ...

'Fo' thirty-three years I kept something special. Very special! That something was a bride-gift I carried in my sandals as a joke to present to the parents of Sisi the girl my son Atu was to marry. An', going, we were captured. Kidnapped and brought here. Well – by some freak of providence I managed to hide, keep an' protect that gift, to travel with it, an' keep it here in Jamaica. An' fo' thirty-three years I keep it!' And taking the two thick plates of gold sheets from each pocket, and holding them up in his hands, Ajeemah went on. 'I present this eventful African bride-gift to this Jamaican Sisi and husband Julius.'

Ajeemah was cheered and cheered. He went on. 'I tell you, this new husband an' wife stay here with Bella an' me, for a while. But, I did get value of this old gift. I hear this gold will buy them own land, an' own house.'

The people could not contain themselves. Everybody wanted to see this amazing surprise of gold, kept secret for so long. The wedding people pressed forward. Some people took the gold from hand to hand and weighed it up and down, groaning astonishment. Some simply touched it, feeling the cold metal. Others merely looked on as if they saw relics from an ancient Egyptian tomb, and kept their distance.

Then the people stood, looking at Ajeemah. They didn't seem to know what to do, how to love him, and honour him, for his depth of endurance and personal loyalty to his past. Obviously overcome by the moment, Ajeemah merely stood there. Somebody began to clap. And everybody clapped, on and on.

It seemed the handclapping would never stop. In the endless hand-burning applause, Sisi began to cry. She had known nothing of the gold. She had known little of her father's painful story. The occasion overwhelmed her and made her ache with an agony of happiness, but also with other mixed-in feelings that racked her with distress. She felt a guilt and a shame. Her father was so strong! So strong! What he believed in and did were of great substance and depth! And her values were so, so shallow! Yet, she preferred hers. She did not like the name Sisi. It sounded too African. And she couldn't help it. Nothing African was popular. She endured the name only because it meant so much to her father. Most people called her 'Emma'. And that was the name she liked. It was the name Emma she liked and wanted and would say her name was. And she would never tell her father. And because of Julius, and her mother's love, and her father's suffering and strength and his amazing surprise gift of gold, and all the people here on such a big, overwhelming day, she wept. And – in spite of all the caring and comforting of the women – she cried on and on.

NEVER MEDDLE WITH MAGIC
AND OTHER STORIES

Chosen by Barbara Ireson

Fifty fabulous stories full of magic and mischief, fun and fantasy. Stories short and long, funny stories, sad stories, 'once upon a time' stories, fairy-tales and ghost stories, birthday stories and Christmas stories — there's something for everyone in this enticing collection.

CHOCOLATE PORRIDGE
AND OTHER STORIES

Margaret Mahy

A sparkling collection of short stories, full of surprises and fun. There's fiery little Mrs Bartelmy, once a pirate queen, who longs for a pet and finds her match in the half-fierce, half-friendly lion; Linnet who overcomes her fear of the swings and seesaw in the playground with a little help from the midnight children, and Christopher who is teased for being a scaredy-cat, and then proceeds to terrify two older boys with a horrible story. And of course there's Timothy who concocts a very special chocolate porridge . . .

STORIES FOR TENS AND OVER

Edited by Sara and Stephen Corrin

What's it like to lead a dog's life? Why did Lady Godiva ride naked through the streets of Coventry? Was it fun to live in Roman Britain? Dip into this selection of stories and you'll find all the answers and lots more to excite your imagination.

THE SHADOW-CAGE AND OTHER TALES OF THE SUPERNATURAL

Philippa Pearce

The supernatural takes some unexpected forms in these ten eerie, gently menacing tales. Like all the best ghost stories, each one suggests more than it says as it unfolds quietly towards its chilling close.